F. W. (Frederick William) Robinson

In Bad Hands

And Other Tales: Vol I.

F. W. (Frederick William) Robinson

In Bad Hands
And Other Tales: Vol I.

ISBN/EAN: 9783337137298

Printed in Europe, USA, Canada, Australia, Japan

Cover: Foto ©Andreas Hilbeck / pixelio.de

More available books at **www.hansebooks.com**

IN BAD HANDS

AND

OTHER TALES

BY

F. W. ROBINSON

AUTHOR OF

" GRANDMOTHER'S MONEY," "NO CHURCH,"
"THE COURTING OF MARY SMITH,"
ETC., ETC.

IN THREE VOLUMES.

VOL. I.

LONDON:
HURST AND BLACKETT, LIMITED,
13, GREAT MARLBOROUGH STREET.
1887.

CONTENTS

OF

THE FIRST VOLUME.

		PAGE
IN BAD HANDS :		
I.	The Lodgers at Broadbrook's	3
II.	Foxy Wharton has his Hair cut	26
III.	What he Came for	38
IV.	Phil Acts for Himself	46
V.	False Security	59
VI.	Disappearance	69
VII.	The Minstrels of the Tyrol	76
VIII.	The Happy Pair	91
IX.	A very Strange Boy	99
X.	The Break-up of the Minstrels	112
XI.	'In Good Hands'	124
MR. BIRD'S BEST UMBRELLA		135
A PRISON FLOWER :		
I.	Child or Woman	197
II.	On Night Duty	208

CONTENTS.

III. The Prison Daisy . . 218
IV. Daisy is Deceived 232
V. The Infirmary Cell . . 244
VI. The Message from the Dead 249
VII. Mistress and Maid . 259
VIII. The Whole Truth . . 280

THE LUCK OF LUKE SHANDS:

I. My Lady's Chapel . . 293

IN BAD HANDS.

IN BAD HANDS.

CHAPTER I.

THE LODGERS AT BROADBROOK'S.

MARSH WALK, in the heart of busy Lambeth, was, at the time of which my story treats, one of the most bustling, struggling, fighting and tearing thoroughfares of the many crowded highways of human life which are to be discovered in South London. The Marsh Walk was always busy; it was a place in which no grass grew under the feet of its inhabitants. It was a squalid place altogether in its way, and they were very poor, 'hand to mouth' folk, who thronged its streets, and haggled for prices at butchers' shops, and begged for credit 'till next Saturday night, sir,—oh! only till next Saturday!'—of the stern man behind the counter, who was selling at the lowest prices the harshest and most alumy of bread, and striving hard himself to live, and failing very often.

Marsh Walk was the highway of the 'poorest poor'—and the shopkeepers were, as a rule, very poor too, to match their customers. Names were always changing over the shop-fronts in Marsh Walk, and only the publicans and pawnbrokers were 'old established' and waxed fat on people's thirst or people's troubles.

One of the poorest shops in this neighbourhood to which we direct our reader's attention was Mr. Broadbrook's—and it was always a matter of grave speculation how Mr. Broadbrook lived and kept house and home together on 'easy shaving at a half-penny' and 'gents and ladies hair cut at three-pence,' or, cut and curled for the sum of fourpence, paid in advance, to save unnecessary disputes, or the fatigue of opening credit accounts.

But Mr. Broadbrook *did* live, and keep house

somehow, and supported, or endeavoured to support, a grimy, and carroty-haired Mrs. Broadbrook and nine small Broadbrooks, all grimier and more carroty than their mother, and whose hair was never cut and curled, and was altogether a reflection on the parent male, a dreamy little man, who passed the greater part of the day in his shirt sleeves, at his open door, with a comb behind his ear, and the handles of several scissors sticking out of the all round pocket of his dirty white apron, like a buccaneer armed to the teeth.

Certainly, Mr. Broadbrook had lodgers, and, *when* they paid their way 'fair and square,' that was a something off the rent, and made up for a paucity of customers. And it is of these lodgers we have to speak; just as the inhabitants of Marsh Walk—especially those living over the way—had spoken, and wondered, and speculated about them for the last two years, and made artful attempts to ' draw out ' Broadbrook, who was not to be drawn out, for the very sapient reason that there was nothing to draw, and the barber was as ignorant as his neighbours.

The lodgers then who rented the small first floor of Mr. Broadbrook, were a woman of some forty years of age, and a boy of eleven or twelve; the woman a pale, washed-out, fragile being with 'not an ounce of strength in her,' Mr. Broadbrook said, and said very near the truth; the boy also fragile, and white as a ghost, with two grey eyes which were several sizes too large for the thin, small face they lighted up so strangely. A quiet pair of lodgers who gave little or no trouble, who had brought their own furniture to the first floor of Mr. Broadbrook's, and settled there for good, paying 'pretty tidy middling' take them the year round, was the verdict of the hairdresser.

No one was expected to pay punctually in Marsh Walk such an out-of-the-way luxury as the rent; Mr. Broadbrook seldom paid his own rent till the brokers were in, when he dunned Mrs. Wharton for arrears, and sold something on his own account to make up *his* quarter. Leave Mr. Broadbrook alone, and he left other people alone, being an easy-going person, as was Mrs. Broadbrook, and as are most poor people with large families, we fancy. If they were not, they would die despairing of the better days, and under the grim surroundings of their lives—as some reckless souls do die in the big city, after all, and glad to get out of it too!

Mrs. Wharton was glad to live and take care of her nephew Phil—though she had not much to be glad about, and it may be said, at first start, that Phil took care of her. There had been times when this was different, but now the position had changed, and one good turn had deserved, and brought about another, as it should do, and as it will do occasionally.

Mrs. Wharton was an invalid, at the period our story opens, one who had almost lost the use of her limbs some time after her arrival at Marsh Walk, and so had been unable to do as much for Phil as she had anticipated when she had taken upon herself his sole care and custody.

'What did you do that for?' asked Mrs. Broadbrook, who was by nature more curious than her husband.

'There was no one else to take care of him.'

'Why not?'

'Well,' was the slow, reflective response, as if such a question took a long time to answer, 'because there wasn't, don't you see?'

Mrs. Broadbrook did not see, but she thought she did.

'An orphan! poor little chap, is he? Ah! that's hard.'

'I didn't say he was an orphan.'

'Bad mother, perhaps—or a father who drinks,' she suggested, without eliciting a response, and adding by way of encouragement to confide in her—'Broadbrook drinks, if he ain't busy, and it's astonishing what a little gets into his head.'

'I dare say it does,' was Mrs. Wharton's broken answer, 'but Phil has not a mother.'

'Oh, I see! that's why you take care of him —whilst the father's away, I suppose?'

'Yes,' she said, 'whilst the father's away— that's it.'

This was not strikingly explicit, but it was all the facts that could be elicited from Mrs. Wharton. And as the father seemed always away, and never came to see his son, or sister-in-law,

and never wrote a line to either, Mrs. Wharton
had no correspondents whatever. The Broadbrooks, and the little circle of hard-workers
round the Broadbrooks, were left to guess at
the facts, or give them up. The missing Mr.
Wharton might be abroad, on foreign service,
in the army, or in gaol, or might even have a
nice little lighthouse to mind somewhere—there
was no telling where he was from Mrs. Wharton's comments on the subject, and the boy
Philip was as reticent as his aunt.

The Whartons paid their way tolerably fairly
for a while, and Philip went to school in the
neighbourhood, and was considered by his contemporaries a quiet, milksop sort of youth, who
stood a lot before he was ' riled,' and then let
out a bit and had his say and held his own on
his little battle-field of life, weak and sickly as
he was. Mrs. Wharton was an artist in wool,
which article, during the first year of her resi-
dence in Marsh Walk, she was incessantly knit-
ting and crotcheting into all kinds of soft goods
that were made into a big parcel once a fortnight, and sent off to a wholesale house near St.

Paul's Churchyard. And it was out of this wool-work that her nephew Philip was supported, for when rheumatic fever seized her, and it was found after a tedious recovery that the use of her hands had not come back to her, the woman and child were in sore straits enough, and had to throw themselves on the mercy of Mr. Broadbrook, who, always in a chronic state of debt and difficulty himself, was not greatly shocked, and said, ' Don't trouble,' in quite a sympathising way, and ' When they begin to bother me, why, I must bother you, and not before. That's all.' And that was quite enough; for the water rate was down upon him the next week, and the gasman, accompanied by a myrmidon in corduroys, cut off and carried away the meter the week following and left Samuel Broadbrook to paraffin lamps and candle dips till the question of arrears was finally adjusted. And they were adjusted by Mrs. Wharton's aid, and by the sale of something or other out of Mrs. Wharton's big box with brass nails—and Philip always noticed that when times were very hard, and the people in them harder, Mrs. Wharton dived into the big box, and fished therefrom something or other that fetched money at the pawnbroker's. Hence there was treasure trove in the corner of her little back bed-room, and it never wholly failed them. It was to Philip's mind an inexhaustible well-spring, till one day there was nothing more to sell, she said, and this at the time when Samuel Broadbrook had the shadow of his landlord's last quarter falling once more across his chequered career like a big black smudge.

It was at this period that our little hero woke up.

'I think I can earn money now,' said Phil, very thoughtfully, one day.

'Not yet, my poor boy,' said his aunt, shaking her rusty cap at him, 'it isn't likely yet.'

'I'm sure I can earn money,' he exclaimed, with a vehemence which scared Mrs. Wharton and took her breath away, her nerves never having been properly under her personal control. 'You see if I can't.'

Mrs. Wharton waited patiently, and did see within four-and-twenty hours, when Philip

Wharton marched indoors with a golden sovereign in his hand and laid it triumphantly upon
the table.

'There, auntie,' he said, 'how about that?'

'Good gracious, Phil, you must have stolen it,'
exclaimed the old lady, beginning to tremble
like a blanc-mange; 'oh! what have you
done?'

'Earned it.'

'Earned a sovereign!   You could not, Phil, it
is not possible.'

'Well, I'm going to earn it,' he explained, 'I
begged for this on account, because you weren't
well enough to do any work just yet, I said, and
we were behindhand with the rent, and getting
hungry.   And the gentleman said, "I don't
believe in boys, but I'll trust you for once," and
gave me that out of his pocket, and—just like a
gentleman, that was, wasn't it?'

'Very much like a kind-hearted gentleman,
indeed, if——'

'Here, I'll tell you all about it.   They've
been talking about my voice, oh, for ever so long,
at school, and pushing me forward in singing,

and I heard old Prouts—that's our singing master—say, " That boy's got a soprano voice that's worth something," and then the choir-master and organist of a church over Westminster way came and heard me a week or two back and said, " What a pity I hadn't been better trained," and made Prouts awful waxy, and then—are you listening, auntie, or going to sleep ?'

' I'm listening to every word you say, but you rattle on so fast, my head's going round and round, Phil,' she said, ' and I don't see——'

' Why, how can you see, when you shut your eyes, Aunt Bella,' he cried.

' Sharp as his father,' muttered Mrs. Wharton, ' well, go on, who gave you that sovereign ?'

' Why, the gentleman at Westminster—the choir-master of St. Eustace's Church,—and he's going to train me and put me in his choir as soon as he can, and I am to have twenty pounds to begin with.   There !'

' Twenty pounds! and at your age !' exclaimed his aunt.   ' Gracious !'

' And perhaps thirty, though he doesn't promise

that. I walked straight to his house to-day, found him, settled the business,' said this small boy, with grave self-confidence, ' and I only wish I'd done it before, when I was a young one.'

Thus it was that Master Philip Wharton became a boy soprano at St. Eustace's Church, Westminster, and being a quick boy, with a voice as clear as a bell, he dropped into a salary that was remarkable considering his years, and became the mainstay, the prop and support, as it were, of the feeble woman struck down before her time, whose one grief was that she was of so little help to him, assuaged by the one comfort perhaps that he was of great help to her, and gave that help with all the warmth of his ungrudging little heart.

And so, from eleven years of age to twelve, did Philip Wharton remain at St. Eustace's and become of grave importance to the choir, and progressed in musical knowledge, under the efficient training he received, and was somewhat a wonder of a boy soprano to be jealously guarded from other choirs and choir-masters who would have snapped him up and carried him away perforce. For choirs are like the myriads in the water drop, and prey on one another. Philip was not elated at his success, and indeed hardly knew he was successful. No one spoiled him by flattery, and the choirmaster, an irritable old gentleman who meant well, but was always finding fault, told him regularly twice a week that he could not sing a bit, and was not worth his salt. The boys were not pleasant company to Phil either, being bigger and stronger than he, and invariably disposed to make game of him when they were not knocking him about, and his only friend was the young organist, Folkestone Miles by name—christened Folkestone by an admiring mother, because he was born in Dover—and a sandy-haired, limp young man by nature he was, who carried his hat on the back of his head, and wore violet-coloured glasses, which were always askew, on the bridge of a long, thin nose. He was a hard working young man, paid sparsely for his duties at the rate of forty pounds per annum, and looking through his spectacles vaguely for extra pupils to make a living for him. He lived or

lodged in Hercules Buildings, Lambeth, and
Philip Wharton, being a little fellow, with a
long way to go from Westminster in the same
direction, often trotted by the side of the
organist, who was not too proud to have him
for a companion, and to ask him many questions,
and to be generally interested in this quiet boy
who had much less to say for himself than
most choir boys have, as a rule.

He was an eccentric young man this Folkestone Miles, and perhaps as curious as the folk in
the Marsh Walk, for the isolation of the lad, his
self-dependence at so early an age, the self-restraint or reticence, which was characteristic of
him, all aroused the organist's interest and
sympathy.

'That boy's a queer customer,' he said to
himself more than once. 'I'll draw him out.'
And, instead of this, it was Master Philip Wharton who drew out Mr. Folkestone Miles, one
sultry August evening when they were crossing
Westminster Bridge together.

'Have you lived in Lambeth all your life,
Phil?' Mr. Miles asked, as they walked on side
by side.

'No—have you, sir?' answered the quiet lad.

'Yes—almost all my life. My father and my mother died in Lambeth.'

'Did they, though?'

'Your father and mother are dead too, Phil, I suppose?'

'Mother is—long ago.'

'Don't you remember your mother then?'

'Oh, yes.'

'And what's your father?'

'I don't know what aunt calls father. Your father was an organist, too, wasn't he, sir?'

'Yes—that's it. Who told you?'

'I have heard you say so before. He was at the same church years ago you told me once.'

'Did I,' said this absent-minded young man, 'very likely I did—I don't remember.'

'Wasn't he very clever at the organ?'

'He was a great musician,' said Folkestone Miles, who would always grow enthusiastic over his father's accomplishments, ' he composed a fugue that should have made his fortune, but it did not. And there's an oratorio in a drawer at home—such a manuscript! If it had only been played anywhere, Phil, I should have been in a different position by this time, but you can't sell oratorios just when you feel disposed. Very few people want to buy oratorios,' he added, ' and nobody wants to hear them.'

' What a pity !' said Phil.

' I have been composing a little myself—but there, you don't want to know what I've done, and it isn't worth while,' he said, ' only I've done no good, Phil, and that's my luck always,' he added, with a pleasant laugh at his own misfortunes.

' Are you very unlucky, Mr. Miles ?'

' To be sure I am ; but it can't be helped.'

' I wish I had forty pounds a year ; I shouldn't think I was unlucky,' remarked Master Phil, with great deliberation.

' Why, you cheeky young rascal, what would you do with it ?'

'Help aunt more.   Help poor old Broadbrook.'

' And help yourself,' suggested the organist.

' No, I wasn't thinking of myself,' said Phil : ' good-night, sir.'

'Good-night, Phil, good-night. Be early Sunday morning, or you'll have the choir-master down on you. He said you were very late to-night. And you mustn't offend him.'

'Did he say that?' said Phil; 'yes, I *was* late. But I couldn't help it.'

'One can always help being late.'

'Not always,' replied the boy, deliberately, and very gravely.

'Why not?'

'Not when anyone's ill, and wants a doctor.'

'Who's ill where you live?'

'My aunt.'

'Why, you haven't said anything about it,' said the amazed organist. 'You didn't tell Mr. Holloboys that that was the reason?'

'No. 1 didn't want to talk of it. Good-night, sir;' and Phil, with his hymn-book under his arm, and his hands in his trousers pockets, walked slowly and thoughtfully away, looking more like a little old man than the boy of twelve that he really was.

The organist glanced after him curiously, stood on the kerbstone of his native street, and watched him through his violet glasses, instead of letting himself into the house with his latch-key, and proceeding to his bachelor quarters on the second-floor back. He grew almost uneasy about the lad; the lad's grave manner that night puzzled him, and suddenly he made a dash after him, and overtook him as he was turning into Lambeth Road.

'Here, Phil,' he said, as he came up with him again, to the boy's astonishment, 'can I be of any use in any way? You're down to-night, and if there's anything I can do, you know——'

'Thank you, Mr. Miles. It's very kind of you,' he answered, looking up very steadily with his great grey eyes at the speaker; 'but no, you can't be of any use to her.'

'Is she so very ill, then?'

'I don't know. I couldn't wait to hear what the doctor said.'

'Do you think she's very ill?'

'She's different like—to me,' he answered.

'Isn't there anyone to write to?'

'Oh, no.'

'Nobody?'

'Nobody.'

'Shall I come home with you?'

'What's the use, sir?'

'Well, I don't know,' confessed Mr. Miles; 'but if you should find out in any way that I *can* be of use, why, you know where I live.'

The boy nodded, and murmured something that was intended for thanks, but which would not come further than a brand-new bung which had suddenly risen up in his throat, and arrested further powers of speech.

With the consciousness that he was rather in the way, Mr. Folkestone Miles turned back, wondering at the boy, wondering a little more what would become of this quiet youth if the aunt were to die, and leave that twelve-year old to begin life entirely on his own account. He wondered at a little more than that, too—why he should be interested in him in any way— having had some years' experience of choir-boys, and being disposed to consider them, upon the whole, as hideous and irreverent tormentors, prepared for any mischief when his back, or Mr.

Holloboy's back, was turned, and doing a fair amount of it on practice nights before his very face.

'But this is such an odd sort of boy,' he muttered, 'a boy who keeps himself to himself. A boy I don't make out, at all, a boy who—oh! bother the boy.'

And he stepped out in double-quick time towards home, resolved to mind his own business, and to brush and do himself up sprucely for a late visit to a pupil—a brush manufacturer's daughter in the Westminster Road, who served in the shop, and had only time for the accomplishments after nine o'clock in the evening, when her father, a rough old savage, sat and smoked opposite master and pupil, and made crude and scoffing comments upon his daughter's five-finger exercises. But, though of limited musical intelligence, she was a pretty, amiable girl, and Folkestone Miles thought a great deal about her, and only wished his receipts were five hundred pounds a year instead of about fifty-eight, take them altogether, and then—Oh! then.

Still it was not nine o'clock, it wanted a quarter to nine, when he was outside in the Hercules Buildings again, with a sprig of red geranium—his own culture from a sooty plant which was perched on his window-sill—in his left hand top button hole, and the boy he had left suddenly rose in his mind again like a ghost not to be exorcised too readily.

'I'll just go into the Marsh Walk and see if it's all right at Broadbrook's. If—if the shutters are down, and the blinds are up, poor little chap,' he muttered, and away he went once more in the direction of Phil Wharton's lodgings, a being possessed with one idea.

Yes, it was all right, and Folkestone Miles' spirits went up seventy-five per cent. for no reason that could be accounted for, or that he, callous being as he thought himself, was likely to own. There was Mr. Broadbrook at the door, serene and smiling and red-headed and hot, with a girdle of bright scissor handles glistening all round his fairly plump waist; there were three little red-headed Broadbrooks, who should have been in bed hours ago, tumbling about the shop, and playing with two razors and half-a-dozen balls of sand soap left promiscuously on the floor, and there were the blinds on the first floor still drawn up to admit into the room all that was left of the twilight lingering in Marsh Walk.

'That's all right,' thought Mr. Miles again as he walked away. But it was not all right, or hardly as right as it might have been.

For if Mr. Folkestone Miles had not been short-sighted, or had his weak vision been unbeclouded by violet glass, which had grown terribly steamy and dull that close evening, he would have recognized, and been surprised to recognize, a burly, high-shouldered, broad-faced, black-muzzled man, who had asked him in Westminster the way to Charing Cross, who had thanked him surlily for the information, and then marched off in a different direction to that which he had been told, who had hung about the church and listened to the choir practice going on within, who had put his head through the doors to listen more attentively, and to peer more closely into the shadowy edifice, who had followed step by step the organist and the boy from Westminister to Lambeth, and who was leaning against the lamp-post at the corner of the street opposite, ostensibly a street figure that was very streety, and was watching furtively from his bloated and blood-shot eyes, as wolves and foxes watch, the windows over the barber's shop, or something beyond the windows of the room in which Phil Wharton and his aunt were sitting.

Aunt and little Phil were as unconscious of the man without, as Folkstone Miles had been. They would as soon have believed in one risen from the dead, as in his coming back; and they would have been less scared at the opening of the grave, and the white figure rising in its cere-cloth, than at encountering face to face that dreadful man again.

CHAPTER II.

FOXY WHARTON HAS HIS HAIR CUT.

ALTHOUGH Folkestone Miles, organist of St. Eustace, had not seen the man at the opposite lamp-post, the man at the opposite lamp-post had taken stock of him, and swung his ungainly and ill-clad body round a little, as if anxious to escape the attention of one of whom he had inquired a short time since the way to Charing Cross. When Mr. Miles had departed after satisfying his mind that all *was* right at Broadbrook's, the man slowly relapsed into his old position, and from under his shaggy eyebrows—which seemed made of wire, so thick and bristly were they— kept his watch again upon the hair-dresser's shop, and upon the hair-dresser himself standing in the cool of the evening on the threshold of the domicile, with a self-satisfied smile upon his countenance.

Presently the watcher crossed the road, and with a solid, heavy slouch moved towards Mr. Broadbrook, who not expecting a customer, or such a customer, gave a little jump of surprise as he stopped in front of him.

' Not too late to have my hair cut, governor, is it?' he said, in a tone of forced familiarity that was particularly out of place in a gentleman so strikingly forbidding.

'N—no,' said Mr. Broadbrook, hesitatingly. ' It's never too late for customers.'

' Very well then.'

' The charge is threepence—in advance,' Mr. Broadbrook added, doubtfully regarding the new comer.

' 'Don't I look worth threepence?' asked the man, as he placed three pennies in the hand of the hairdresser forthwith.

' Oh yes, but it's the rule of the establishment.'

Mr. Broadbrook backed into his shop, and

over his sprawling children, set a chair for his visitor, and enwrapped him with much briskness and sleight of hand in a grey cotton sheet that had only been a week from the wash, and was less dingy than might have been expected.

'Run away, my chicks,' said Mr. Broadbrook to his progeny, ' You see, papa is engaged,' and, at this suggestion, the three young Broadbrooks scrambled off the floor and departed like dutiful children to another sphere of action. Meanwhile the customer for hair-cutting sat with a very much battered, billy-cock hat on his head as though there was no necessity to remove it.

'Will you allow me——' said the hair-dresser at last, with a suave movement of the hands in the direction of the hat, and the man who was staring absently at the fireplace in the shop, and the hot shaving water ready on the hob for any-one who might want an evening ha'porth, said nothing in dissent. Mr. Broadbrook removed the hat gently, turned up his one jet of gas, and produced a pair of scissors from his apron with an easy flourish. Then he paused and looked down on his customer's head of hair, with a certain amount of curiosity and awe. He had seen a great many heads of hair in his time, and had operated upon them fearlessly—and masculine heads of hair in Marsh Walk were of all degrees of tangleness and picturesque confusion —but this particular crop was uncommonly and luxuriantly wild, and matted together so strangely that even Mr. Broadbrook was perplexed how to make his first start, and in which direction.

'Fine weather for the country, sir,' he remarked, as he hovered in the rear with comb and scissors prepared for immediate action.

'Yes,' hastily assented the gentleman in the chair, 'fine weather.'

'Been in the country lately, sir?' Mr. Broadbrook ventured to remark, as he became aware of the various grassy filaments mixed with his customer's hair, and which were strongly suggestive of the gentleman having slept last night under a haystack.

'I came from the country yesterday. I have been there for the benefit of my health,' he added, with a sudden, mocking laugh which had no sense of fun in it.

'Oh! indeed.　Harvest all in, I suppose?'

The man writhed in his grey wrapper as though Mr. Broadbrook's questions were annoying him, and then growled forth—

'I don't know.　And I don't care if it isn't.'

'No—ahem—I suppose not.　How will you have your hair cut, sir?　Long or——'

'Anyhow,' he answered, without waiting for the operator to finish his sentence.

'Oh.'

'You don't think it matters a great deal in what particular style I have it cut,' he said, in a friendly tone, as if suddenly aware that civility of demeanour would become him better, 'do you, now?'

'Well—we always like to know.'

'I was particular enough when I was a young fool, but I've got over all that nonsense now.　So, Mr. Broadbrook, I leave it to your taste.'

'Very good, sir.'

Then the little barber attacked him in earnest,

and struggled hard with comb and scissors, the customer groaning very often, and cursing now and then between his strong, white teeth, which would have been a redeeming feature in his personal appearance, had they been a little less in size than dominoes.

Presently when he was out of pain, and there was a considerable portion of his hair shorn or torn away, and lying on Mr. Broadbrook's sanded floor, he said:

'You must find it uphill work to make a fortune here, Mr. Broadbrook?'

'Fortune is not the word, sir. A living it is —nothing more.'

'And you get a living out of this. Really?'

'Really,' repeated the hairdresser, not disposed to run down his own position in society before so rough a customer, 'and a fair living too, as times go.'

'Ah! you're lucky,' remarked the man, as if he doubted him; 'I don't see how it pays myself. I could put you in a way of earning money a bit faster.'

Mr. Broadbrook did not respond. He did not

like the manners of the individual whose head he was, as he inelegantly termed it, ' licking into shape,' and though they were exceptionally good manners for the gentleman under treatment—company manners, in fact—they had failed to make a favourable impression on the hairdresser.

After a moment's silence, and imagining Mr. Broadbrook had not heard him, he repeated slowly :

' I could put you in a way of earning money a bit faster than this. Don't you hear ?' he added, sharply : and after another moment's pause, ' Where's your tongue got to all of a sudden ? You were talkative enough a minute ago.'

' I don't want to earn any money,' said the hairdresser, tetchily.

' Oh, don't you though ?'

' And you will excuse me, but you look as if *you* did.'

The man scowled at Mr. Broadbrook, as though he resented this flippant and uncalled-for observation, and the hairdresser felt an unpleas-

ant creeping up his back, at the darkling glance
bestowed upon him. Mr. Broadbrook was not a
brave man, and, as a rule, not personal, but the
impudence of some people, he considered, would
make a worm turn, and hence his natural affabi-
lity had changed suddenly to pertness. He was
a London shopkeeper in a big thoroughfare—one
who paid his rent and taxes pretty regularly—
and to be 'talked to' by a common rough,
emphatically a rough, was a little too much for
his equanimity.

Nevertheless he wished he had not taken any
notice of him and his remarks, after encountering
that terrible sidelong glance from the man
swaddled up in the grey wrapper. It told of a
creature who was dangerous—of a wild beast to
be on guard against, he was pretty sure of that.

The best thing to be done, was to get him
out of the shop as speedily as possible, and to be
as civil as possible to him also until he had gone.
This was a fellow out of the common—or out of
the jungle—and Mr. Broadbrook had not discovered that fact a moment too soon.

The man seemed to read what was passing in

the hairdresser's mind—being with all his crude-
ness, his suppressed desperateness, a man of an
observant turn—for he made another effort to
laugh pleasantly, and turned Mr. Broadbrook all
goose-flesh in the futile effort.

'Money-making never was in my line,' he remarked. 'I've had my chances, and lost them,
like a good many more people. And I don't
complain, do I?'

'No, indeed. Dear me. Certainly not,' replied Mr. Broadbrook, willing to agree with his
customer on every point now.

'What's the good of complaining after the
chance has slipped out of one's hands? Do you
see any good in that?'

'No, I don't.'

'Then you're a philosopher. Come over the
way and have a drink?'

'N—no, thank you,' stammered Mr. Broadbrook, 'I—I never drink in business hours.'

'That's a lie,' was the flat contradiction here.
'You came out of the "Jolly Gardeners" three
quarters of an hour ago, wiping the back of your
hand on that slobbery mouth of yours. I saw you.'

'I—I went to see the time,' explained Mr. Broadbrook, and yet wondering why he said this, as if by way of an apology. And he *had* popped across the road with that object, and the landlord had in the most friendly spirit asked him if he would—'just a drain,' and he had 'drained' accordingly, at the liberal expense of a liberal but improvident host who was fast draining himself into his grave by undue consumption of the stock-in-trade.

'I don't want to force anybody to drink with me,' said the man, making another effort to be conciliatory, after his impromptu burst of energy. 'I've plenty of friends too glad to get drunk at my expense. Even *you* don't find friends of that sort scarce, I reckon?'

'Oh, dear, no, certainly not,' assented the barber, with a feeble chuckle. 'There's lots of that sort about, and no mistake.'

The man's hair was cut, but he still sat there, wrapped in Mr. Broadbrook's cotton toga, as though he had found the hairdresser to be pleasant company, and was very loth to part with him. He could not expect to sit there all night for threepence, and talk in that queer, scoffing way like a man who had had his better days, and been a fool in them; and Mr. Broadbrook hoped in his heart another late customer would step into his premises and oust the present party from them.

'There you are, sir, unless there is anything else I can do,' said Mr. Broadbrook at last, and whisking the wrapper suddenly from the stalwart form before him.

The man looked at him from his half-shut, crafty eyes, and, with a smile that was as bad as his laugh had been, said,

'Do you think I look nice and smart now?'

'It has certainly improved you.'

'Fit for the society of ladies, eh?'

'Why not?' rejoined Mr. Broadbrook, lightly, and yet not committing himself to a palpable untruth.

'And why not?' was the echo back. 'Then, Mr. Broadbrook, be good enough to inform your upstairs lodger—your " first-floor front," as you would call her—that her brother Foxy particularly wishes to see her.'

'Bless my soul and body!'

'And that he's not going away without seeing her,' added Mr. Wharton, as his big teeth closed together with a clashing sound, 'and if he stops here till doomsday. You may as well mention that to her as well whilst you are about it, Broadbrook.'

CHAPTER III.

WHAT HE CAME FOR.

MR. BROADBROOK remained speechless for a few
moments, and regarded Mr. Wharton with eyes
distended, and his lower jaw reposing on his
chest.

'Mrs.—Wharton's—brother!' he gasped forth
at last. 'I—I didn't know she had a brother.'

'She's a close one. Miss Wharton—or Mrs.
Wharton, if she likes it better—always was a
close one,' replied Mr. Wharton. 'Don't you
see a likeness?'

'Can't say I do, although, now you come to
speak of it——'

'Tell her, will you?' exclaimed Mr. Wharton,
very roughly now. 'Do you think I can wait
here all night talking to you?'

Mr. Broadbrook was scared by this fierce inquiry out of his own shop into his back-parlour, where was Mrs. Broadbrook, to whom he communicated the news in a stage whisper, and making many excited danger-signals with his arms.

'Go up and tell her, Charlotte, he's come.'

'Who's come?' exclaimed his better half.

'Her brother—a regular blackguard—had his hair cut—wants to see her—ask her to tell you whether I shall show him up, or send for a dozen policemen to take him away. Look sharp.'

Mrs. Broadbrook, looking sharp in consequence, hurried upstairs to the first floor, and her lord and master skipped into the shop again, where he found his customer examining a small regiment of razors ranged in a row against the wall, taking one down after another, and feeling the edge of each with a very black, thick thumb.

'Well, what does she say?' he asked, as the hair-dresser reappeared.

'Mrs. Broadbrook has gone upstairs with your message.'

'I asked *you* to go,' he growled forth. 'Women always muddle messages.'

'Mrs. Broadbrook is a much better hand at messages that I am; and I never leave my shop till the shutters are up,' the hair-dresser added, with a faint assumption of dignity.

'Except when you go over to the "Jolly Gardeners,"' said the man, with a shrug of his broad shoulders. Then he put the last razor back, and began to walk round the shop slowly, reading all the bills upon the walls, the programmes of the 'Surrey' and 'Victoria,' the grand attractions at the 'South London' and the 'Canterbury,' the wonders to be seen nightly at 'Gatti's' and the 'Winchester,' the 'friendly lead' at the 'Malsters' Arms, in Gravel Lane,' the annual summer excursion of the Lambeth Undertakers to Box Hill, the terms for a quarter's instruction at the dancing academies down various back streets in the vicinity, the forthcoming great cricket-match at the Oval, and a 'prompt' sale by auction of the goods and chattels of an unhappy neighbour, too far gone in arrears of rent to do anything but be sold off without reserve.

Mr. Wharton had read all these announcements before Mrs. Broadbrook came into the shop : his impatience had vanished again and 'he seemed to take it awful easy,' thought the hair-dresser. He was in no hurry now—quite the contrary.

'And how's the boy getting on, Broadbrook ?' he asked, as he turned away from the last specimen of wall literature with which the shop was decorated, 'how's Phil ?'

'Oh ! he's pretty well,' replied the hair-dresser, ' works hard, and gets on, I should say, famously. A nice little fellow.'

'I am glad to hear you say that. Thankee, sir—thankee.'

'He ain't—is he—' began Mr. Broadbrook.

'My only son, sir. Yes. And what a sweet voice he has—and how it tells at St. Eustace's. Have you heard him sing ?'

'I should think I had,' exclaimed the hair-dresser, 'not at St. Eustace's, for it's a goodish way off, and Mrs. Broadbrook takes the young ones to the chapel round the corner, in the afternoon, when it isn't too hot ; but of course we have

all heard him. We sit on the stairs, one behind
the other sometimes, and listen to his singing,
his practising, you know. It's beautiful—one
wonders where it comes from—he's a wonderful
little chap, take him altogether.'

'Yes. That's why I'm so proud of him,' said
Mr. Wharton.

'Oh! you are?' replied Mr. Broadbrook, 'Oh!
indeed.'

'I don't miss a note of his voice every Sunday. I can pick him out of the whole lot of
them, like a winkle. I can——Oh! here's somebody at last.'

Mrs. Broadbrook emerged cautiously from the
back parlour into the shop, and approached Mr.
Wharton almost on tiptoe.

'She's very ill——'

'What do I care about that,' cried the man,
flaming out again, 'what's that to do with me—
what's——'

'Gracious, man, let a body finish,' exclaimed
the barber's wife, starting off herself in a higher
and shriller key, 'but she'll see you, if you wish.'

'All right. I do wish.'

'Then go upstairs, and don't make too much noise or you'll wake my baby,' said Mrs. Broadbrook, 'it's the first floor front room.'

'I know,' answered Wharton, nodding his head as he strode past her into the parlour, and through a side door leading to the stairs, up which he clumped his way in heavy, thick-soled boots, covered with a week's mud, which had dried upon the leather in a white and nubbly pattern. On the first landing stood a pale-faced boy holding in his hand a small oil-lamp to light the footsteps of the visitor towards him—a boy with eyes too large for him now in very truth, dilated, as they were, with horror at the man's approach. The coming of a phantom from another world could not have scared young Phil Wharton more than this coming of his father, who from another world too—a world of sin, and shame, and devilry, beyond one's power to describe—advanced towards him like an ogre.

'Phil,' said the father, in a rough grating voice, as he caught sight of him on the landing, 'so you're there then.'

'Yes,' was the soft, low answer back.

As the father approached, the son, light in hand, went slowly backwards through the open doorway keeping his great grey eyes fixed upon the visitor, and then, step by step, into the room and to the side of his sick aunt, sitting in a pillowed chair by the fireplace, with two thin hands crossed upon her lap, and her white, lined face, turned steadily towards her brother as he entered with that scowl of hate she knew so well, and had fled from, years ago. And yet, with him before her again, it seemed only a day or two since she had stolen away, taking his child with her, saving his child from him.

Phil put the little lamp on the mantelpiece, and then stood by his aunt's side watchful, and calm, and pale, and Foxy Wharton looked from one to the other as he closed the door carefully behind him, and turned the key in the lock, as though doubtful or afraid of those who might follow in his wake.

Mrs. Wharton was the first to speak.

' I did not think I should see you any more in life, Mark,' she said, calmly. ' I had a hope that you were dead.'

'A pretty hope that was,' answered the man, 'so nice and kind too! I'd have been ashamed to own as much as that to anyone. Well, I haven't come to see *you*—I could have lived on or died off, without fretting myself about you, Bella, very comfortably.'

'What have you come for, then?'

'*For him!*'

And Mr. Mark Wharton, better known amongst a choice circle of friends and acquaintances as Foxy Wharton, stepped across the worn-out hearthrug, and laid his big broad hand upon the shoulder of his son.

CHAPTER IV.

PHIL ACTS FOR HIMSELF.

Phil Wharton shrank for an instant beneath the heavy hand of his parent, and then recovered himself and looked his father steadily in the face.

'I can't leave aunt,' he said.

'We shall see about that,' Mr. Wharton answered; 'you go and sit down there whilst I talk to your aunt a little while. I hate listeners. They're dirty sneaks.'

'Phil need not stay at all,' murmured Mrs. Wharton.

'Oh, yes, he need,' was the flat contradiction proffered by her brother. 'Do you think I have taken all this trouble to find my only child—the long-lost son, feloniously abstracted from my house and home—to have him slip away again. Thank you, Bella dear, but I'll keep him in sight, please.'

Phil sat down by the window—which was still open that hot summer night—and looked into the street below. He was very pale, but very grave and self-possessed. It was impossible to guess what thoughts were troubling him, or distressing him, by. a glance at his quiet little face. They were shutting up some of the shops in the Marsh Walk now; all the drapers and all the 'fancy goods' depôts for wooden dolls and tin soldiers and detonating balls were closed; the greengrocer's, the hot-baked sheeps' heads emporium, the cheesemonger's next door, and the oil-shop were still expectant of customers, though they had lowered their gas to half-cock : the tobacconist over the way was actually busy with three youths, the tallest having resolved to try one of ' Brown's famous penny smokes,' and his two companions having accompanied him to superintend the purchase and make sure that Mr. Brown picked out a

nice and mild one; and the 'Jolly Gardeners'
was a blaze of light and life, with two per-
formers, with violin and piccolo, playing at the
jug and bottle entrance, the piccolo with his left
eye riveted on the landlord behind the distant
counter.   There were some drops of rain patter-
ing into the street, and covering the pavement
with black spots, and the policeman across the
road was telling the master butcher next to
Brown's that it would be a wet night, and very
good for the country, if not for him upon his
beat. ·Phil could hear the words, and he wondered what kind of night it would be for him
now, and how it would end, with Foxy Wharton glowering at him there, and his aunt endeavouring to look calm and undismayed, and
hold her ground against her brother.

Mr. Wharton had taken a seat and was leaning a little forward on the chair making his
intentions as plain as possible to his sister, and
emphasising his discourse by various slaps on
the table with his brown, hard hand. He had
been always, even in his best days, a noisy brag-
gart, Mrs. Wharton was aware, and therefore

his manner was not new to her, and did not in any way surprise her. She remembered it too well—she, and the poor wife who had died young, and got away from him, had grown very used to it once upon a time. And here was the grim, dark time back again, as it were, and these three face to face again without any friendly greeting, any token of the strong tie of kindred existent between them, any loving looks or fair-spoken words. Nothing but fear and distrust, and a wonder in the woman's mind, as in the boy's, as to what would come of it all.

The man was endeavouring to make that clear enough to them; but his listeners were not disposed to agree with him, only to speculate already as to what would be the result of opposition to his wishes, even to the extent of a direct defiance of them.

He spoke of the law, and laid before them the law's opinion, which they did not believe. He had been all his life too lawless himself to impress them very much in that way—hence his legal knowledge, his exhibition of virtuous in-

dignation, might, under less serious circumstances to them, have bordered on burlesque.
But now in their hearts they were simply afraid
of him. They had run away in fear of him some
years ago, and the fear had grown no less.
That night had even added to its strength.
This was a crisis in their career which they
thought might come some day, although the
man had never cared for them, and might
possibly have been very glad to get rid of them
for what they knew to the contrary. Why
should he want to see them?—they had been a
clog upon him always, and he had always looked upon them as very much in his way, and told
them so, and swore at them for the encum-
brances they were. They had not credited him
with any paternal instincts, and yet, after all,
there he was before them asserting his rights
to be considered the lawful guardian of his son.

'What use would he be to you?' inquired Mrs.
Wharton at last.

'Never mind what use. That's my business,'
replied her brother; 'and it's high time I looked
after him, and saw his education was not being

neglected.   How do I know in what way the boy has been dragged up ?'

' He has been well looked after,' was the slow reply. 'He will make a better man, Foxy, than you have been.'

' I don't want any sauce,' Mr. Wharton replied. ' You always had a nasty, biting tongue of your own, and that's what got you so generally disliked.   And I'll thank you not to call me "Foxy;" it's a vulgar nickname, which I repudiate.'

' You were rather proud of it once, I used to think.'

'Pity you hadn't something better to think about,' said her brother ; ' to think, for instance, how that dear boy is going to get on in the world after you are gone—and you don't look as if you'd last the blessed week out—or of how you reconcile your canting talk with running away with my property.   What have you done with that ?'

' It was Mary's own property.   It belonged to her mother.   It has been used to keep Phil alive.   Mary gave it me, when she begged me

E 2

to escape with Phil, at any risk and cost, to get away from you.'

'It's all very well to tell me that. It's a poor excuse, and I don't believe a word of it,' he said.

'It's the truth.'

'It's a clear case of kidnapping and wholesale felony. What do you think the police would say to the whole business?' he inquired.

'Call in the police and ask them.'

'Shan't. I am not so fond of them. I can manage my own business, thank you. So, Phil,' (in a loud voice), 'get on your cap, and come with me.'

'Where?' asked Phil, quietly.

'Never *you* mind where,' roared the man; 'that you'll find out in good time. I'm your father, and there's no one here dare stop me—no one to prove he has the faintest right to stop me ; so come on.'

'And aunt, who has been so good and kind to me since mother died—who has been so like the mother to me?' murmured the boy.

'Rot your aunt!' he exclaimed. 'I'll have

nothing to do with her; and I'll train you up to hate her presently.'

'Oh, no, you won't.'

'What's that you say?'

'You can't do that, father; that's not in your power.'

Mr. Wharton looked hard at the boy, whose pale face was set and resolute, and whose grey eyes did not flinch from the fierce light they met in his. He wavered, and then changed front. 'I mean,' he said, 'when you know all the truth which she's kept from you, boy. When you and I are in the country together, living like lords or fighting-cocks, and happy as the day is long, with no work to do, and yet the money coming in, nice and regular, Phil, and only the two of us to spend it. When——'

'I can't go with you.'

'But you must go.'

'I can't trust you again. I'm afraid of you as —as mother was,' said Phil. 'I recollect what you were before we ran away. I can't forget all that.'

'Here, I've stood enough of this!' he shouted.

What were Mr. Wharton's intentions were not very clearly manifested, although he had sprung to his feet as if with the object of carrying off his son by sheer force of arms—not so difficult a task, perhaps, considering those with whom he had to contend, and 'the rights' which were on his side. He could not go to law, perhaps, for the recovery of his child, but there was no one to go to law with him—no one to whom this mighty, sluggish law would listen, if Phil were once in his possession.

Bella Wharton saw this, and the boy's instincts were keen enough to second her. In his father's power he was surely helpless. Foxy Wharton had been so terrible a sire—so irredeemably bad and callous and unjust—and life with him again was to live the life of the lost. Woman and child had striven hard to get away from him, and this was too miserable an end to all their efforts.

Phil seemed to have only one chance of settling the question that night, and that was to get away as speedily and swiftly as it had been done before. At all events it would postpone the question for that evening, and save further disputes and much violence of language. Phil stepped suddenly out of the window, amongst the flower-pots, and went lightly along the narrow ledge of shops to Hickman's the cheese-monger's next door, where there was a shop-blind still running out across the street, and an iron bar thereto supporting it, festooned by Ostend rabbits. The instant afterwards Phil Wharton was dangling amongst the rabbits, and the instant after that he had dropped to the ground, bringing down a rabbit or two with him, frightening the man in charge, and scaring Mr. Broadbrook almost out of his life, and just as he was gingerly putting up the last shutter of his establishment.

'Bless my soul and body, what's the matter now,' exclaimed the hairdresser, as he slipped down, shutter and all, on the wet pavement in his consternation.

'Don't say which way I've gone. Be good to aunt, please,' cried Phil, as he took to his heels—and a very light pair of heels too—along the middle of the Marsh Walk, sending up a

fountain of mud over himself as he ran. Mr.
Broadbrook gathered up himself and his shutter
and looked vacantly after Phil's retreating
figure till he was once more swung round by
an opposing force in the huge shape of Mr,
Wharton, who came tumbling out of the shop
and upon him.

'Which way has he gone?' he cried out.

'Which—way—has—who gone?' asked the
barber, staggering about with his shutter very
helplessly.

Foxy Wharton did not stop to explain. In
the distance he could see Phil running swiftly
along, and he set up a whoop of 'Stop thief,'
which roused the echoes of the street, and
enlisted attention and auxiliary forces at once.

'Stop thief' set all Marsh Walk alive. It
always did. The place was a common hunting-
ground for the vagrant and the desperate, and,
though this was a cry patent to the neighbourhood, it always aroused interest and excitement
and 'fun.' Mr. Broadbrook put up his remaining shutter and then joined in the race on his
own account, and in the hope of being of some

service should Phil be overtaken, and the cheesemonger's young man followed with alacrity, believing that he was a rabbit short, and not stopping to count his stock in hand in the eagerness of pursuit.

But when Foxy Wharton, and his band of volunteers, and the hairdresser, and the cheesemonger's young man had turned the corner of the street down which Phil had plunged, there was no sign of the youth who had taken flight, and all was damp, and dark, and desolate in James Street. Conscious of this fact, after a while, Mr. Broadbrook went speedily homewards, before Mr. Wharton had recognized him, and bolted and barred his premises for the night with an extra degree of precaution.

He would sit up for Phil, nevertheless, being sure that he should see him later on, and hear him knock quietly at the door for re-admittance, which would be granted after a few inquiries through the key-hole, and the making sure that it was not Foxy Wharton who had returned. He went upstairs along with his better half, to talk it over with the aunt, who had 'quieted down,' she said, and was very glad that Phil had got away—and very sure, like Mr. Broadbrook, that Phil would quickly be back again.

' I shall see him soon, and then we will talk over what is best to do,' she said.

But she never saw Phil Wharton again, and there was no talking it over in this world for her.

CHAPTER V.

FALSE SECURITY.

THE next day there came a letter to Mrs. Wharton, care of Mr. Broadbrook, hairdresser, 729, Marsh Walk, and the letter was from her nephew Phil, and ran as follows :—

'Hercules Buildings,
'Lambeth.

'MY DEAR AUNT,

'I got away stunning! But it was not till I was clear off that I found out I had twisted my ankle dropping from old Hickman's blind. Tell him I am very sorry, and hope the rabbits did not get much damaged, and if they did, I will pay for them some day. I fancy you gave me the office' (*tipped me the wink*—the boy

had written in true boyish slang, and then had
crossed it out again, at the suggestion of a
friend to whom he had shown the letter before
despatching it) 'to get away; and it was jolly
easy to slip out of the window and drop into the
street. I am afraid I dropped upon Mr. Broadbrook, as he was shutting up the shop; but I
don't remember anything, except seeing him
sitting upon the wet pavement, with the shutter
in his lap. My love to him, and I hope he isn't
hurt. I am quite safe with Mr. Miles the organist,
who is going to keep me in his house, and out
of the way, until my ankle is better, and I can
get about again. He is a regular good one'
(*brick* had been erased, and good one substitut-
ed), 'and won't let me move off the sofa ; and
hopes you will not fret about my being absent,
or let father worry you again, if you can help it.
You will do as well as you can without me, and
keep nice and cheerful. I hope to get to church
next Sunday. Mr. Miles·thinks it would not be
safe for you to come round to me, as father may
be watching the shop in Marsh Walk, and follow
you. I miss you very much. My best love, and

please feed my silkworms, which you will find
inside my Sunday cap, and I should like my
prayer-book and hymn-book sent by post, and
don't worry about me, and get well soon, and
God bless you, auntie, and with love to you, and
all the Broadbrooks,

'Your affectionate Nephew,
'PHILIP WHARTON.'

'That's a good boy, to think of all those who
are anxious about him,' said Mr. Broadbrook, to
whom the letter was slowly and gravely read
by Mrs. Wharton; 'I'm very glad he's written.'

'You will not let my brother know where Phil
is, if he should call again?' said the old lady.

'Madam, I would rather welter in my own
gore, in my own shop, slain by his own hand,'
answered the brave Broadbrook,

'Yes, it would be better,' remarked Mrs.
Wharton, absently. 'Thank you—you are very
kind.'

But there was nothing seen of Foxy Wharton
in Marsh Walk, and the opportunity to defy
that gentleman was not offered to Mr. Broad-

brook. Still, the house was watched, and a very thin, shabby, collarless man, deeply pitted with small-pox, took an interest in the wares displayed in the shop window, and gazed at them admiringly half an hour at a time, despite the stock consisting only of pomatum pots, a few combs and brushes damaged by the sun and the flies, and seven bottles of 'Broadbrook's Three-penny Rose-Oil for the Nursery,' a bright crimson fluid which the nurseries of Marsh Walk sternly refused to patronize, although there was nearly half a pint for threepence, and the colour was absolutely dazzling.

This thin man of shabby exterior, 'with a face like a cribbage board,' as Mr. Broadbrook described it afterwards, was evidently keeping an eye upon the premises, and was not to be frowned away by the proprietor. When tired with gazing in the window he would take up his position by the lamp-post, where Mr. Whar-ton once stood, or hang around the doors of the ' Jolly Gardeners,' dropping in occasionally, like a man with drink money to spare, and very often thirsty. Mr. Broadbrook took counsel of a

policeman, who did not see what was to be done,
and recommended Mr. Bradbrook's applying to
the police station in the Lane, where the hair-
dresser was snubbed by the inspector and told
to mind his own business, and to wait at least
till something illegal *had* happened before he
began harassing the authorities with his cock-
and-a-bull stories.   As for the father, why, he *was*
the boy's father, and nobody denied it, and
there was nothing to be said against him that
anybody could prove, and Mr. Broadbrook
and his female lodger had better be careful
they did not get themselves into trouble presently for keeping the boy away from his lawful
guardian.   Just what Foxy Wharton had said—
and said with emphasis; and Mr. Broadbrook
returned to his shop in Marsh Walk in a desolate
frame of mind, and with a dim prospect of
standing in the dock by the side of Mrs. Wharton, to answer a charge of kidnapping.

But the lawful guardian did not claim the
assistance of the law. The name of Wharton
was unknown to the police, but there were
several aliases by which he had been known,

and might be still inquired for, and it was as well to manage matters his own way. And his own way was to take possession of his son, and bring him up to be a comfort, *and* a source of profit to him.

And we may say at once that he was perfectly aware what had become of Phil, and with whom he was staying. He had not followed Phil Wharton from the church of St. Eustace, Westminster, to his home in Marsh Walk for nothing; he had seen his son in company with the organist, and noticed him shake hands with him at the door of his lodgings; and it was Folkestone Miles to whom his suspicions were first directed when it was discovered that the choir-boy did not return to his aunt Bella.

The nets were closing round this little stray, though he was unaware of it, and Folkestone Miles, as well as himself, was buoyed up by false security.

' It is all right, I think,' the organist said on the Sunday morning, when it was very much all wrong, and Phil was able to limp, if a little slowly, across Westminster Bridge to the church of St. Eustace and sing his very best there. In the evening Mr. Miles, always thoughtful and considerate, and warm-hearted, treated him to an omnibus ride to Westminster, and thought, he said laughingly, that it would 'run to it' on the homeward route again; and Phil's heart warmed to the young man as towards an elder brother, and life would have been pleasant and happy with him had it not been for the thoughts of his aunt, patient and hopeful, and always waiting for him in the upstairs room at Broadbrook's.

'The house is watched—you must not come home yet,' she had written to say, forgetting, or rather not guessing, that Mr. Miles's house was watched as well, by men determined to have this singing-bird, and seeing the way to make it worth their while. Had Foxy Wharton been captain of the forty thieves he could not have been served more faithfully by the subordinates about him, and two of them were even inside St. Eustace's itself next Sunday evening, outwardly devout, and inwardly watching and plotting for the boy's capture. They sat in the free seats, and listened to his singing, clear and bell-like, and of surprising power; they nudged each other craftily as they noted the effect upon many of the congregation to whom the choir of St. Eustace was the principal attraction, and prayers and sermon only a secondary consideration, if even of any consideration at all; they crept out of the church before the service was quite finished and lay in ambush outside, in the shadows of the vestry, trusting for the chance which might present itself, and for which they had planned. For which they had prayed too, —understanding such prayers as that, and knowing nothing of the earnest supplications they had listened to, in church that night, making neither head nor tail of them.

It was by cruel chance that the vicar of St. Eustace called Mr. Folkestone Miles back into the vestry that evening, when the choir had gone its various ways, and Phil was about leaving with his friend.

'I will not keep you a moment, Mr. Miles,' said the vicar, blandly, and Mr. Miles, nodding to Phil, and implying by that nod that he was to wait for him outside, passed into the vestry with the clergyman, and Philip went on, recking not of danger by the way.

The vicar was not quite as good as his word, and the minute became two, three, five, lengthened even to ten before all had been explained about a special service which was due on Friday next. When Folkestone Miles was in the open air at last it was lightening vividly, and through his violet glasses he could see no sign of the chorister. Phil had grown tired of waiting, he thought, and had gone slowly in the direction of Hercules Buildings, unmindful of the ride homewards that had been promised; and Folkestone Miles stepped out, confident of overtaking him before the Houses of Parliament were reached.

But he failed to come up with him, or his weak sight had not stood him in good stead, or he had passed him, or the lightning, which was very blue and vivid, had confused him on his way. He was not nervous about Phil, even when he found that he had reached home before the boy; he was a sharp walker, and of course had passed Phil, who was very lame just then— it was only half-an-hour afterwards, three-quarters, and then an hour, that there came to his slow mind the suspicion of foul play.

CHAPTER VI.

DISAPPEARANCE.

FOLKESTONE MILES sat up all that night waiting and wishing for the coming of little Phil, but the choir-boy was seen no more in Hercules Buildings, Lambeth. He had vanished like a ghost—leaving, ghost-like also, not a clue by which he might be tracked. Those who had trapped him had managed their nefarious business neatly, and had vanished as completely 'into thin air' as the boy whom they had captured. Over the whole affair hung the black curtain, heavy and thick and pall-like, and there was no drawing it aside and seeing where Phil was. He was gone and for good.

He came not back to the organist's home; he

was seen no more by Aunt Bella who, pale, ill, and patient, was sure every morning that she should hear of him before nightfall, possibly see him; and thus buoyed up for a while her poor vain hopes, though growing weaker every day along with them. Folkestone Miles, restless and excited, called twice a week to see her, to ask if there were any news, to talk it over downstairs with Mr. and Mrs. Broadbrook, and speculate with them concerning the great mystery, all three making wild guesses at the truth.

'He must be dead,' said Mr. Broadbrook on one of those occasions; 'he would have surely found time to write, to let us know somehow where he was. Depend upon it, sir, that boy is dead.'

'I don't think so,' remarked Mr. Miles.

'Murdered probably. If ever I cut the hair of a murderer for threepence I cut it that blessed night he kicked up such a row here,' said the barber.

'It was not worth while to take all that trouble to murder Phil,' said Mr. Miles.

'Perhaps there were estates coming to him,' suggested Mrs. Broadbrook, who had been reading 'penny dreadfuls,' in large quantities, and was a little weak in mind in consequence.

'Yes, but who would have benefited by killing Phil?' said Mr. Broadbrook, critically.

'The usurper,' was his better half's confident reply.

'Who's he—that father of his!' cried the barber, with a disparaging elevation of his nose. 'Well, he didn't look much like one to me; although I must say I never saw a real usurper to my knowledge. What's he like, Mr. Miles?'

Mr. Miles found it extremely difficult to describe off-hand an usurper's personal appearance and said he did not know for certain. From a histrionic point of view, he thought it was something in black velvet with a point lace collar.

'Well, the boy's murdered,' said Mr. Broadbrook, firmly, 'you see if he isn't. You wait.'

'We shan't see—and we must wait,' replied the organist, as he walked away thoughtfully.

And seeing nothing and waiting in vain became the order of the day in Marsh Walk and Hercules Buildings, and with never a gleam of light to show the track through the mists. Mr. Broadbrook's neighbours talked of it for a time and then dismissed the subject; the choir-boys wondered and wondered for a week or two, and then almost forgot that Phil had ever lived; the choirmaster, a sceptical man, half believed there had been an underhand plot to smuggle Phil off to another church at an advanced rate of wage; and the vicar, still more sceptical, was quite sure of *that*, for it was an old trick; the police laughed their heads nearly off at the station-house, and could see nothing alarming in a boy's going away with his own father, and without the ceremony of a formal farewell to a sleepy old aunt, and one or two people who seemed to know very little about him.

And so time drifted by, and the hot, close, summer in Marsh Walk became the cooler autumn which presently drifted into the mild, wet winter for which that year was famous,

even in crowded Lambeth, where the difference
in the seasons is noted by the goods upon the
costers' barrows rather than by any changing
tints or fall of leaves, and the days which
' draw in,' as the phrase runs, are only regulated
by the longer scores upon the dials of the gas-
meters. And later in the winter Bella Wharton died and was buried by the parish, and Mr.
and ·Mrs. Broadbrook officiated as chief
mourners, and shut up shop to do honour to a
lodger who had died very much in their debt,
and yet with whom these wonderful folk were
sorry to part. And later on still Mr. Broadbrook got more deeply into debt himself, and
discovered that his landlord was a more
merciless creditor than he had been to Phil's
aunt; for the brokers swooped down in earnest
upon him at last, and out went the barber, his
wife and family in a strange hurry, and were
seen no more in Marsh Walk or parts adjacent.
' I wonder what's become of old Broadbrook,'
one or two people said at first—the landlord of
the ' Jolly Gardeners,' who missed a good customer, for one—and then the world spun round

and there were fresh faces in the crowd of struggling men and women, and ' Jones, Dealer in Second-hand Wearing Apparel, and Ladies' Wardrobes purchased,' was printed over the premises, and announced in the windows where 'Broadbrook's Rose Oil for the Nursery' had offered its attractions to passers-by in vain.

To round off this portion of our little story we may chronicle another change, although it did not happen till late in the spring, when there were wall-flowers on the barrows, and green-peas could be got for sixpence a peck from the costermonger, if one were inclined to put faith in a measure the bottom of which was pushed upwards when the peas were put in! Mr. Folkestone Miles left the church at Westminster ' to better himself,' went in for a competition for an organist's post at a fashionable church further west, and got it, even to his own astonishment, not being quite certain whether he was a clever fellow or not, but inclined to think at times, and with a due amount of modesty, that he was not quite a fool. Hence Hercules Buildings knew him no longer, and the last of the characters of our story passed away from Lambeth, and, unlike the rest of them, began to prosper a little and to gather round him by degrees various well-paying pupils in the new neighbourhood in which he had pitch-ed his tent. So whilst some folk went down others went up, in the see-saw fashion patent to humanity.

CHAPTER VII.

THE MINSTRELS OF THE TYROL.

A CLEAR twelve months after the disappearance
of Phil Wharton, there was bright summer
weather down at the pleasant watering-place of
Tenby, in South Wales. The old town was
full of company; in the memory of the oldest
inhabitant there had never been so prosperous
a season, and the north and south sands were
equally thronged with visitors amusing themselves, or being amused, working hard at sand-
digging, cavern-exploring, fossil-hunting, energetic bathing, and desperate donkey-riding, or
taking it very easily in lazy, happy groups of
loungers and sprawlers on the sands, or in the
Castle grounds, listening to the Tenby band, or

those itinerant musicians whose mission in life appeared to be to take the bread out of the mouths of the Tenby band by vigorous competition, and who had been lured thither on this occasion by the news of Tenby's doing well and being very full of company—of Monmouth and Cardiff folk, of Swansea swells, of the 'fat of the land' from Birmingham, Manchester, and Liverpool, of the families from London, with time and money to spare for the long journey, and for settling down afterwards, of the tourist from everywhere with his clattering bicycle, tricycle, sociable, or, better than all, with his own sturdy legs to carry him up or down fair mountain-side, stiff path, or valley, where anything on wheels would surely come to grief in this nubbly quarter of the kingdom.

Into this romantic old Welsh watering-place there tramped one bright morning a band of singers and players who styled themselves the 'Minstrels of the Tyrol,' for no particular reason that was apparent, one man being a German, another unmistakably French, and the rest as thoroughly English as anyone could wish—unless it was in a faint attempt at a costume which might by a stretch of imagination be set down as Tyrolese, and which consisted of steeple-crowned hats, green cotton velvet jackets and knee-breeches, and tricolour ribbons dangling from their shoulders and knees, and from the rims of their weather-beaten felt hats.

They were eight in number, one man not a singing member of the corps, but a burly gentleman who wandered about with a highly-polished shell, which was presented to each visitor who stopped to listen, and who, having contributed to the expenses of management, was rewarded with a bow so elaborate and profound, and with a grin so wide and alligator-ish, that the suspicion that all this was a burlesque of gratitude instinctively occurred to the donor.

Nevertheless the 'Minstrels of the Tyrol' became popular favourites at Tenby, and were rewarded by so many sixpences and shillings that the rumour that they were coining money began to circulate amongst the visitors. They became the favourites of the place—as itinerants will, under certain favourable conditions, and with some talent to raise them above the street standard of howling vagabonds—and their entertainment on the sands became extensively patronised, and was considered 'quite the fashion' to attend between the hours of twelve and one.

These minstrels were clever in their way: the Frenchman was an expert violinist, who played on his instrument upside down, and fiddled away with extraordinary rapidity and precision; the German was a flautist of ability, and a third man worked the violoncello, less effectively perhaps, but with a knowledge of time and tune that kept him in accord with his contemporaries. The remaining few were part-singers, and the chief attraction of the company; three voices were a little above the average of men singing out of doors for a living; but the fourth voice was of surprising sweetness and volume, a remarkable boy soprano voice, that took listeners off their guard and entranced them strangely. It was a voice out of the common run indeed, and led to innumerable inquiries of the man

with the shell, who shrugged his broad shoulders
and showed his big white teeth, and thanked
everybody for much advice and friendly suggestion, and gave everybody as much information
as time would allow concerning his 'leetle son,'
speaking in the broken English of his native
Whitechapel; but imposing on a few folk, credu-
lous and unsuspicious.

'Filippo Moriega was a clayver boy—a goot
boy—yes, he should be trained by great masters
soon some day—to be sure. That's what he
(Ludovic Moriega) was saving for—taking a
troupe round the country for—to make money
to give Filippo—Gord bless him!—a musical
education at Rome. Indeed, they were making
their way to Rome now, the whole of them,'
Monsieur Moriega, senior, affirmed, as though
Rome was somewhere round the corner, and
South Wales was indubitably the nearest way
to it.

Filippo said very little himself, and it was
found difficult to say anything to him; he
remained always in the centre of the singers
and players, a thin pale-faced youth, with large

grey eyes and a very sad and thoughtful expression in them—a youth who walked with a crutch, and that with considerable difficulty, it was observed.

'What a pity he is a cripple,' said many a sympathizer amongst the crowd which the 'Minstrels of the Tyrol' drew about them; and 'Has he been a cripple all his life?' was often the inquiry put to Monsieur Moriega, who answered, 'Ya'as,' unless his questioner looked medical, when he said, 'No, sa'ar,' with equal confidence, before he bowed himself from too many questions which might become irksome and inquisitorial. It was observed that none of the minstrels cared for too much questioning: they were in Tenby to sing and play, not to give autobiographical sketches of their career, and at times they were so haughty and reserved that a few romantic minds had spread about the notion that they were foreign noblemen in disguise, Italian refugees or Neapolitan wreckage, or a something or other wrapped in mystery, although the maestro of the company was of the full proportions of an English navvy, and looked far more bulgy than aristocratic, in his green cotton velvet smalls.

It was one hot August morning, when the 'Minstrels of the Tyrol' were playing and singing to a large audience on the south sands, that a lady and gentleman, attracted by the crowd and by the part-singing which was going on just then, left off walking hand-in-hand, in a slightly silly and sentimental fashion, and strolled towards the centre of attraction.

' Something in your line, dear,' said the lady.

'Yes, my darling love, so it is,' replied the gentleman.

The affectionate couple stood at the back of the crowd and clasped hands together again, then the gentleman who wore violet glasses on his nose, and a straw hat encircled by a broad blue ribbon on the extreme back of his head, rose on tiptoe and endeavoured to peer over the heads of the audience, and failing in his manœuvre, being short of stature, to gain a clear view of the singers, began jumping about like a sportive kangaroo.

'My dear Folkestone, whatever is it?' exclaimed the lady, alarmed for the sanity of her brand-new spouse and helpmate—not married more than forty-eight hours to him either, and coming all the way from Westminster Bridge Road, where the wedding had been celebrated, to this picturesque portion of South Wales to spend the honeymoon.

'What's the matter? Oh, dear! what is it? Is it a fish-bone? Won't you tell me?'

'It's all right, Fanny; it isn't a bone in my throat—it's the voice—it's—it's that boy!' he exclaimed, incoherently, and continuing to jump.

'In your throat—a boy! Oh, Folkestone! what *do* you mean?'

'It's Philip Wharton—you know—the missing lad. I'll swear it is, by thunder!' exclaimed the excited organist. 'Fanny, we must part!'

'Oh, mercy!'

'For a few minutes—perhaps for half-an-hour, or till dinner-time—don't fret; don't stop me—please let go the pocket of my jacket, Fanny, or I shall rip—I must know all the truth!'

And with a sudden dive into the crowd, unprepared for so unceremonious an attack in the rear, Folkestone Miles plunged his way into the front rank, and stood glaring through his glasses at the singers, deaf to the objurgations and protests of several ladies and gentlemen, astonished, shocked, and indignant at his rudeness, and hurling 'Well-I'm-sure's' and 'I-never-did's' on all sides at him. But he paid no heed to them—did not even hear them.

Yes, that was surely Philip Wharton! Little Phil, of Marsh Walk—the lad who had been spirited away from him, carried off twelve months ago almost to the very day. But Phil did not recognise him, although he stood exactly in front of him, and Folkestone's glasses should have been a landmark and reminiscence. Folkestone could have run forward and shaken hands with him—even have hugged him to his breast in the joy of the discovery; but a second and wiser impulse warned him to be careful. If it should be necessary to get Phil away from them, if Phil was a prisoner and anxious to escape, if he had not joined this band of singers and players of his own free will—he, Folkestone Miles, must not let any excitement betray him to this crew. He would simply stand there direct in front of Phil until he was recognised by the lad. There would be plenty of time to act afterwards, he thought.

But Phil did not recognize him. Gentlemen in neutral-tinted glasses, blue, violet, or black, were not uncommon in August by the seaside when the sun's glare was powerful, and Phil had got used to them now, although they had made him start more than once in the grim, early days of his strange wanderings. And the present Folkestone Miles was so wholly unlike the little, shabby, rusty black-frocked young man by whose side he had trotted in the old Lambeth days, that he could not associate the organist of St. Eustace with a straw hat, a 'blazer' jacket—red and green—a pair of baggy, flannel trousers, and sand shoes of a dazzling yellow. That was a festive figure, foreign to Hercules Buildings and the life within fifty miles of it. This was holiday time, and there had been no holidays in Lambeth for Folkestone Miles any more than for Phil Wharton.

The boy glanced once at him from underneath his broad felt brim, and went on with his singing calmly and unconsciously, and the thought that he might be mistaken crossed the mind of the organist. Phil was not so tall, not quite so pale and thin as that, and not a youth scarcely able to put the tip of one foot to the ground—the crutch was against him, and the costume, and the place in which he was. But that voice, thought Mr. Miles, with his ears attuned to music very keenly, and with a memory for voices that had music in them preternaturally strong, was it possible he should be deceived? Phil's was an uncommon voice, too; he had had strange dreams of what Phil's voice might turn out one of these fine days if it were cared for properly and duly trained; it had been, as a soprano in a church choir, a remarkable voice; it was on these bright sands, and with a sea-breeze interfering with it, still more remarkable that day.

Yes, it must be Phil; but why did not Phil recognise him as readily as he had recognised Phil, thought Folkestone Miles, not taking into

account the extraordinary 'character' of his
tourist suit, and the complete disguise it was to
him.   Presently an idea seized him; he would
beat time with a copy of that day's *Birmingham
Post*, which he carried in his hand.   He had a
demonstrative way of beating time, and the
choir-boys had often giggled at it, when he had
been called upon to act as deputy in the choir-
master's absence, and Phil had laughed too, or
sat and stared at him with wonder when he was
extra energetic, which had occurred more than
once in his lodgings in Hercules Buildings.

Folkestone Miles rolled up his newspaper, and
began, to the evident astonishment and disgust
of the Tyrolese; there was a little tittering
amongst the community around him; 'a musical
enthusiast,' said one, and 'drunk so early in the
morning—dreadful!' was the verdict of the
charitable majority. When he had executed a
particular flourish with his extempore bâton, and
stamped wildly upon the sand—sending a dense
shower of gritty particles over a basket of very
sticky tarts which a youth was purveying round
the inner circle—the boy, Filippo Moriega, or Phil

Wharton, turned suddenly very white, dropped his crutch, and left off singing.

It was only for an instant, but Mr. Miles knew he had been recognized, although Phil was strangely impassive the instant afterwards, and went on singing very calmly, as though nothing remarkable had occurred to disturb his equanimity.

Folkestone Miles left off beating time, put a shilling into the shell which Signor Ludovic Moriega presented to him suddenly, with his usual bow and broad grimace, and with an extra keen look at him from head to foot, as at an object of great interest. Folkestone backed his way out of the crowd, and rejoined his anxious wife, who was inclined to reproach him, and to sob upon his shoulder in the light of day.

'I—I didn't think you would desert me like this—and so soon too,' she cried.

'My darling, you don't understand,' said Folkestone Miles.

'Oh! why did I leave home?'

'My precious one—haven't I explained? Don't

you remember all about little Phil Wharton?' he exclaimed.

'Phil who?'

'Phil Wharton, of Marsh Walk—the choir-boy!'

'Yes—yes. I think I do. But *is* this—this a time—to be running after dirty boys!'

'My dear Fanny, we must save him. We—they're going. Good gracious!' And away darted the excitable organist again, as the crowd separated, and the minstrels one by one plodded across the deep sands towards the High Street. The boy with the crutch was the last of them, and Folkestone had increased his pace, to get to his side, and say a few words, when the big fellow, like a shabby cotton-velvet brigand as he was, suddenly strode back and took up his position on the right of his son, clutching at Phil's arm, dragging it through his own, and glancing back at Folkestone Miles, who was stealthily approaching.

'Who are you looking after?' he asked.

'Nobody.'

'Yes, you are. I know that man,' Foxy

growled in the ear of his offspring, 'and so do
you. So take care what you're about, do you
hear? or it will be the worse for you.'

CHAPTER VIII.

THE HAPPY PAIR.

FOLKESTONE MILES did not intrude, after all, upon the society of Foxy Wharton and his son that particular morning on which he had discovered Phil. Discretion was the better part of valour, he thought—the better part of a great many things besides valour, if he were going to act as Phil's champion or deliverer. Through his violet glasses he perceived that the boy thought so also—seemed even to warn him not to speak, and as effectually, by the droop of his shoulders and drag of his gait, as by the very forbidding scowl which he had received from Wharton senior.

Making up his mind suddenly to a new and

distinct line of policy, Folkestone Miles marched past them both at a smart pace, and went home, thereby leaving, he hoped, some doubt in the mind of Wharton *père* whether there was anything more in him than in the ordinary sea-side lounger. He did not know, however, that Mr. Wharton, one practice night, had followed him and Phil from the church of St. Eustace, Westminster, to Hercules Buildings, taking stock of him all the way, and remembering him always from that time by his thin, pale face, his long hair, and the coloured glasses to his spectacles. He had a fallacious idea that Phil's father had never set eyes upon him before, and, therefore, that he would be able to act presently with considerable success.

Mr. Miles returned to his sea-side lodgings to find Mrs. Miles in grief and great tribulation of spirit. She had not settled down to married life yet, and the vagaries—she could call them nothing better than vagaries, she said—of Mr. Miles had very seriously disheartened her. It was like absolute desertion to have Folkestone flying all over Tenby after minstrels of the

Tyrol at a time when she had a right to expect—even demand—his sole and undivided attention.

'It's—it's not a bit like a honeymoon,' she cried behind her white pocket-handkerchief. 'I was never treated so in all my life. It's dreadful!'

'My precious!' he said, soothingly.

But 'my precious' was not to be soothed too quickly by endearing terms, and it was only by appealing to her feelings, by telling the story of Phil Wharton over again from beginning to end, by gently and delicately reminding her that they might have a dear child of their own stolen away some day, and with no human soul to help them find it 'ever and ever again,' that the exciteable young bride became interested in the case, and thought that Folkestone might be excused his eccentric conduct of the morning.

'We will save him, Folkestone,' she said at last, 'but we will save him together.'

'Well, we'll try, at any rate,' answered the bridegroom, though he did not quite see the way to begin, not being blessed or cursed—which is it?—with a particularly fertile imagination.

They must wait and watch, they both considered. The Tyrolese would not, probably, leave the town whilst business was brisk. Mr. Wharton was strong on the point of law, and on the point of possession, and it was difficult to know how to act until Folkestone had had a little talk with Phil. Poor Phil! he thought, walking about with a crutch, and evidently a cripple for life—poor Phil, a prisoner in bad hands, and unable to escape from them! 'By Jove, he shall escape though!' cried the organist.

Folkestone Miles and his young wife made many inquiries that day concerning the Tyrolese; they found out that they were lodging in the small house of a bibulous fisherman, down a back street near the pier—'all of a lump, like a lot of pigs,' said their informant—and that they were not particularly amicable amongst themselves after business hours, and were heard quarrelling and swearing and shouting long after their more peaceful neighbours were in bed and trying to sleep. Once the Frenchman was heard crying 'murder,' but as he

turned up on the sands in the morning, smiling
and gesticulating as usual, it was set down as a
little pleasantry on his part during the previous
night. And once Mr. Moriega was heard striking something or some one with a strap, and it
was thought it might be his little son, as he did
not sing the next day, and was at home with
toothache, 'poor little fellah,' the father explained, with a deep sigh, to those who had missed
him and inquired after him.

The general opinion of the working-classes
of Tenby—those who knew the Tyrolese in
their hours of leisure—was that they were a bad
lot, and the sooner the town was rid of them,
the better. 'If the swells only knew what a
gang they were, they wouldn't pitch their
money at them quite so freely,' was the verdict
pronounced, but the swells *would* pitch away
their money, and the Tyrolese were surely pros-
pering, although there was nothing to show for
it particularly, except some straggling figures
reeling homewards late at night down the narrow, shadowy street wherein they lurked.

'This makes my blood boil, Fanny,' said the

organist at supper—in their smart first-floor lodgings on the North Cliff—and flourishing his knife and fork bravely above his head; 'the boy is kept a prisoner—treated badly—half-killed— I'm sure of it.'

'Yes, dear—but please don't shout so. They'll hear you in the road.'

'And perhaps they are watching us, my darling, as we are watching them,' he said.

'Oh! don't say that, Folkestone, you make me so dreadfully nervous. Hadn't we better shut the windows?'

Fanny Miles left the supper-table at once and approached the French windows, opening on to a balcony, where this happy couple had intended to sit lovingly and quietly day after day and watch the great green, restless sea, and the oyster boats sailing in and out with the tides, and the white gulls scudding from cliff to wave, and from wave to cliff again, and the happy pleasure-seekers wandering below them and not half so happy as they were. The clock in the tower of the old church was striking eleven as she stepped timidly on to the balcony and peered down into the dusky road. They were living at the upper end of the town, and the place was very still and quiet at that hour—the lapping of the sea upon the sands and the soft murmuring of the summer wind alone broke the stillness of that starlit night. There was only a light here and there behind the blinds of the houses in the terraces sloping towards the pier—people were tired and had gone to roost, and there was but one living soul in the far distance—a primitive-looking policeman, grey-bearded and bent a little askew, who was toddling along in the middle of the road, with his little cane in his hands like an antediluvian 'masher.'

'I had no idea it was so late,' said Fanny, 'I had no idea—— *Yah!*' she shrieked out, dashing back, all legs and wings, into the drawing-room, bringing the heart of Folkestone Miles into his throat, and curdling every drop of blood in his body. 'Mercy!—save me!—fire!—thieves!—help!' Then she fell into the arms of her lord and husband, and hid her head upon his manly waistcoat.

'My dear, what is it? Pray compose your-self,' he entreated, 'how you've frightened me! —I've run the fork through my upper lip—what is it? Pray don't kick, my love! what can——'

'The balcony. Somebody creeping up it! oh, shut the windows!' she screamed; 'for heaven's sake lock the windows, Folkestone, we shall all be murdered.'

'No—no—wait a moment! Don't shut me out, oh! don't shut me out,' cried a shrill voice, and then Phil Wharton, capless and shoeless, and with his velvet jacket torn across the arm, where he had encountered a nail in climbing up the trellis-work beneath the balcony, tumbled into the room and ran panting and scared to-wards his old friend.

CHAPTER IX.

A VERY STRANGE BOY.

'Phil—my poor Phil,' exclaimed Folkestone, 'you have got away then. How did you get here? Where's—the crutch?' he asked, after a moment's hesitation.

'I haven't got it. I don't want it,' exclaimed Phil, speaking very hurriedly. 'May I draw down the blinds? It's safer.'

Folkestone nodded, and Phil ran back and pulled the blinds down before the windows. Meanwhile Mrs. Miles had been deposited in an arm-chair, and was slowly recovering from her alarm.

'To think you've got away,' said Folkestone, shaking hands heartily with Phil, 'and now— and now—what are we to do with you?'

'I haven't got away yet,' cried the boy. 'I have only come to see you, Mr. Miles.'

' But——'

' But let me speak, please, sir. I haven't much time. I want to get back before they miss me. Don't you see that?' he said.

' I don't see anything very plainly,' answered the bewildered organist.

' I am so glad to find you—to know you are here and will help me presently. I am so glad!' Phil exclaimed again ; ' it's the old times come back to see you—the dear old times in Lambeth when you and I——' and then a lump rose in Phil's throat and he could not get on any further.

'Take it more quietly, boy. Sit down, there's a good fellow, and let us understand the position, and what is to be done. Where have you been all this while?' asked Folkestone. ' What have they been doing to you that you never wrote to us, or sent any of us a line ?'

' I wrote as soon as I could get the chance ; there was no chance for months ; and the letters came back to the address I'd put upon them.

You had all gone away, my aunt, Mr. Broadbrook, you.   I wrote to all of you.'

'When was that?'

'Six months ago—nearly.'

'Yes,' said Folkestone Miles, thoughtfully,
'we had all gone then.'

'Your aunt——'

'Yes, yes, I know, sir.   Don't tell me again.
She's dead,' he said, sorrowfully.   'They knew
that soon afterwards, and they told me, thinking I should settle down amongst them, having no one to care for and to fret after any
more.'

'And why did you not write earlier?' asked
the young wife.

'I'll tell you as soon as I've got my breath,
ma'am,' Phil replied, and Mr. Miles noticed that
he was still panting from his recent efforts
to approach them, and looking considerably
exhausted.

Folkestone poured him out a glass of ale,
which he sipped at and then set aside again.

'It has struck eleven, hasn't it?' he asked.

'Yes.'

'I must be back before twelve. Before *he*,' he added, with a shudder, 'comes home.'

'Your father,' said Mr. Miles, interrogatively.

'Yes—my father,' he replied.

'The wretch—the awful wretch,' cried Folkestone, indignantly.

'Yes, he *is* an awful wretch,' said Phil, with grave deliberation, 'that is, everybody says so. But we won't speak of him just now, please. There isn't time.'

'Well—well,' said the organist, 'it would take a long time to reckon him up, I daresay. How did you fall into his hands? How did I manage to miss you on that night, Phil?'

'I'll tell you in a moment, sir,' said Phil, hurriedly, 'and then the whole story another day when—when I'm safe. For,' he added, lowering his voice to a whisper, as though there might be eavesdroppers in that very house, 'I am not safe at present.'

'I hope you are, boy.'

'No, not yet,' he answered, sadly, 'it has not come yet.'

'What hasn't come?'

'The chance of getting away from them. They would follow me—they would kill me.'

'We'll see about that,' said the organist, with a cheery laugh. 'Kill you, indeed!'

But the boy did not laugh in return, only stared at the speaker with his great eyes.

'They were waiting for me outside the church that night,' said Phil, by way of explanation of last year's disappearance. 'That's how they got hold of me, although I struggled very hard. There were two or three men, and there was a cab ready to pitch me into, and to be driven away with me. They were determined to have me, Mr. Miles, and that's how it was done. They hid me in a house in a street that seemed somewhere near St. Eustace, for we weren't long in getting there, and then they found my leg was broken. You may remember, Mr. Miles, it was not strong just then, and in my struggles it snapped.'

'Poor little chap,' said Folkostone, sympathetically. 'Here, take some more beer, do. And the doctor—didn't the doctor——'

'They never sent for a doctor. That would

not have done. One of them had been a medical student, and he set my leg, after a fashion.'

'And crippled you for life?'

'Almost. Although,' he added, sinking his voice to a whisper again, after the new habit he had contracted with the wild beings amongst whom his life had been lately spent, 'I am not so bad as they believe. I don't want the crutch, but I pretend I do, so that they shall fancy, sir, I can't move without it; and every night they take the crutch away, and think I'm safe.'

'I see. That's pretty cunning for a young one, that is,' said Mr. Miles, admiringly.

'I have been amongst cunning people,' answered the boy, frankly; 'and I haven't improved. That wasn't likely, was it?'

'Well, no.'

'I have dropped awfully down. But I'll get back again—I will, sir, if you'll help me,' cried Phil.

'Why, of course I'll help you.'

'Thank you. I didn't know. Everybody has seemed so much against me that I didn't know how to trust in anybody.'

'Poor fellow.   Take some more beer.'

'No, thank you,' said Phil; 'I won't have any more of that, or I shall go home like father, drunk,' he added, with another visible shudder; 'and when he's drunk he's very dreadful. At his worst then—always.'

'I don't doubt it in the least,' said Folkestone in reply.

'For six months I never got a chance, night or day, of writing to anybody, of telling anybody, how I had been snared,' Phil Wharton explained further. 'When I was well enough to leave my bed and limp about, they took me away, and we went from town to town earning our living, as you see. My father never let me out of his sight; it is only lately he thinks I have got used to him, and not likely to escape. And I did not know where to escape to when the letters came back and you were all gone— every one of you! I gave up then. I should not have minded them killing me for trying to find one friend; I should have been glad enough to die and get it over.'

'And now you are going to live, and grow

famous, perhaps. For it's a wonderful voice, Phil,' said the organist; 'and something must be done with it soon, instead of wearing and tearing it all to pieces with those singing scoundrels.'

'That's what father says.'

'Your father appears to have studied the matter very deeply,' said Folkestone Miles, caustically.

'Yes, and he's proud of me, after his way,' said Phil, to his listener's surprise. 'Sometimes I think he even cares for me a bit—as a father should, I mean. But,' with an odd little sigh. 'I suppose that's all fancy.'

'Most likely,' assented Mr. Miles.

'Though he lost his voice when he was young, he seems to know as much as you do about music, Mr. Miles—and I haven't gone back in that,' he added, with a hollow little laugh. 'It would have been better for me if I had.'

'Why?'

'They would have turned me adrift then, I think,' Phil answered; 'and I should have got back to London, and found some of you.'

'Perhaps you would.'

'How's Mr. Broadbrook, and Mrs. Broadbrook, and all the rest of them?' he asked, with all a boy's eagerness for news; 'you know, I daresay.'

'They have gone away. I don't know what has become of them,' was the reply.

'And you—married?'

'Yes, and down here for my honeymoon, Phil.'

'You're a—bit—better off than you were then?' he inquired, with some delicate hesitation.

'Yes. I have a better church, and I have five-and-twenty pupils.'

'I am glad to hear it,' said Phil; 'I wish I was one of the pupils.'

'So you shall be—if you will.'

'Yes, presently—who knows,' cried Phil, with his eyes sparkling at the prospect, and then becoming full of thought again; 'some of these days, I hope.'

'And now, what is to be done?' asked Folkestone, 'will you stop here and defy them? Shall I ask the landlady to take care of you, to hide you? They'll never guess you're here.'

'Oh, yes, they will! They know who you are, and they can easily find out, as I have, where you're lodging. Father knows you very well. He said he should probably cut my throat if I had anything to say to you,' said the boy, coolly.

'Oh, good gracious!' exclaimed Mrs. Miles.

'But he always talks like that; that's his way, ma'am,' said Phil, apologetically, on his sire's behalf.

'And a very nasty way of talking too. Folkestone,' to her husband, 'he had better not go back. What is the law about it?'

'Smothered if I know,' replied Folkestone, rubbing his hair up the wrong way in his perplexity, 'and I don't much care. I'm going to defy the law.'

'There's a dear,' said Mrs. Miles, admiringly; 'I thought you would.'

'Yes, Phil, you had better stop. We could get away in the morning.'

'No, we couldn't,' said Phil, who seemed to possess the most practical mind of the three, 'they would watch this house and watch the station. That's why I have come—to ask you to take no more notice of me yet awhile, to leave me with them just the same—to let me be quite sure of the next step before I make it. In the night like this I can come again, to-morrow or the next night even, and tell you what I have arranged.'

'You talk as if you hadn't quite made up your mind to get away,' said Folkestone, regarding him for the first time somewhat doubtfully.

'I think I have; oh! yes, I'm sure I have.'

'They treat you badly.'

'Yes, they treat me badly, most of them,' he added, with a reserve.

'And life much longer with them means going utterly to ruin.'

'Yes, that's it,' assented Phil.

'Then you must get away.'

'Yes, I will get away,' said the boy, starting to his feet, 'and you will help me. That's arranged, unless——'

'Unless what?'

'Unless anything should happen. They might

find me out coming here. I might die ; there are such lots of things to stop me, after all. But,' he cried, 'I am so glad I've seen you, and found you well and happy. I am so very glad. God bless you and this lady, sir ; and thank you both for thinking of me. Good-bye.'

And, without a moment's further hesitation, Phil shook hands with them, darted to the window, drew up the blinds, and passed through to the balcony, over which he climbed and dis-appeared. Always very handy at climbing and getting in and out of windows, this Phil Wharton.

Husband and wife went to the balcony and watched him speeding along in the shadow of the houses, and looking very unlike a cripple at that moment.

'He's keeping something back,' said the organist, 'he seems almost loth to leave them at the last.'

'Poor boy, he is confused.'

'I should not be surprised if he stops with them, for some reason or other.'

'Impossible.'

But it seemed as if Folkestone Miles was not very far from the truth in his new and startling surmise. At the same time the next night, when the town was still and most folk seemed to have locked up and gone to bed, Phil Wharton came like a cat up the trellis-work again, and through the window left open to receive him. He came in looking very white and scared still.

'I have altered my mind, sir,' he said; 'don't think the worst of me. But I'm not going to leave them.'

'Not going to leave them, Phil!'

'No, sir. I can't.'

CHAPTER X.

THE BREAK UP OF THE MINSTRELS.

WE can more easily and briefly explain the mysterious behaviour of Master Phil Wharton by looking in upon the home of the 'Minstrels of the Tyrol' on the morning preceding Phil's second visit to the Miles's. The minstrels were seriously depressed, and yet nervous and excited; there was trouble in the house of Wharton, or in the house which they temporarily occupied, and it was considered that Foxy Wharton was 'not quite himself' by a very long way indeed. It might be even said that he was 'beside himself' with rage, being a man who took any little ailment with great discomposure of mind and spirit, and broke into much bad language under any affliction with which he might be visited. If there was one thing more than another which put him out completely, it was the fact that he was not feeling as well as he could wish. And he liked to feel well and strong, with a grand capacity for eating and drinking—especially drinking, which he always thought agreed with him.

Yesterday he had not been first-rate—qualmish, in fact, with shivers. And now all day he had been troubled with a splitting headache, and, possessing a large head, there was of course more ache in it than there would have been in people's heads of less abnormal development. He had come home very drunk the night before and quarrelled all round with the members of his band, and knocked down the German for screaming at him in a foreign language he did not understand, and had thrown himself on the floor to sleep in a somewhat excited and heated condition. There he must have caught cold and cramp, for he woke up with this headache, and with pains in his joints and with no appetite, and with most unpleasant swimmings, and a general inability to make use of his limbs—all of which signs of bodily prostration he anathematized freely, and raved over, and wondered at.

Still he was determined to go out with the minstrels as usual that morning. There was no one whom he could trust to collect the money, and he was not going to be robbed at his time of life, just when a little more prosperity, and an opportunity of drinking more freely, had presented itself, thanks to a liberal public. But, when he rose to put on his felt hat, he found a difficulty in walking, and the first half dozen steps into the street were accompanied by such a formidable attack of 'staggers' that he sat down on the pavement to consider the question afresh, and to look helplessly up at the seven dusky faces looking down at him.

'Have any of you fellows been trying to poison me?' he asked, suspiciously. 'Have you, Phil?'

No. No one had been trying to poison Foxy Wharton. No one had dreamed of such a thing. The German, who had been knocked down last night, thought it was not at all a bad idea, but it had not suggested itself to him before.

'I can't go any further,' he groaned; 'help me up, and take me in again.'

'Shall I run for a doctor?' asked Phil.

A doctor! Mr. Foxy Wharton here expressed his mind, firmly, strongly and most fully upon doctors in general, declining their interference, and threatening to kill, or gouge the eyes out of the first medical practitioner who came to do him any good, or even to so much as look at him.

Take him indoors, and let him rest; he should be better before the morning was over. He was only a bit queer on his legs—spasms, perhaps, or indigestion.

They helped him into the front parlour, and put him on an old sofa there, which did duty as a bed for five of them during the night, Phil and the two foreigners sleeping in the room above, when there was a chance of sleep, Phil's father being fond of late hours, and cards, as well as ardent spirits. It had been a dispute over the cards which had led to blows last night; they were at it when Phil had returned from the organist's to his lodgings, and gone up to his room *viâ* the zinc waterspout outside.

'You chaps go and do your best without me. And don't keep any of the money. I know what it will come to pretty well,' he said, 'and I'll look you up later on, I daresay.'

'All right.'

'And, hi!—here—Phil will stop with me,' roared forth Mr. Wharton, 'he sha'n't stir a step.'

A blank look of dismay settled on the countenances of the itinerants.

'We can't do without him. We sha'n't get any money without him,' grumbled the spokesman—a shadowy figure in our story whom we have once seen cowering in the back seats of the church of St. Eustace—an old friend of Foxy's, and a man who spoke his mind at times —a prime mover in the capture of Phil Wharton twelve months since.

'I tell you he sha'n't go,' shouted Mr. Wharton, 'isn't that enough?'

'You can trust him with us,' said the man, persistently, 'we can see after him as well as you. We're not likely to let him go, are we?'

'I'll keep an eye on him myself. He stops here,' cried the father.

'Very well, then we'll all stop,' was the obstinate reply, and the musicians unpacked their instruments, and pitched their felt hats into a corner, and the German, with a strong want of consideration for the headache of the manager, began tuning up his double-bass.

Mr. Wharton looked at them indignantly and then doubtfully, and finally, to their amazement, when they had settled down, and taken out and lighted their pipes, and filled the little room with tobacco smoke, he burst into tears and began to moan and gesticulate like a big child.

'Blest if he isn't going soft,' exclaimed a minstrel; 'what's the matter now, Foxy?'

'To be treated like this—after all I've done for you—you infernal vagabonds,' he cried, wringing his hands, 'I won't stand it—I can't stand it! Phil, reach me something off the mantel-piece to throw at them. That flat iron will do.'

'Phil better not do anything so seelly,' muttered the Frenchman.

'Take him with you then—get out of the place, let him run away and ruin us, as he means to do. I know—I know all about it. Get out all of you, before I go mad looking at your cussed ugly faces,' he went on, whimpering and raving, 'just leave me to myself.'

The men rose, and prepared once more for their exit. Phil went to his father's side.

'I would rather stop with you,' he said.

Mr. Wharton scowled at him, and dried his tears with the back of a huge dirty hand.

'What's that for?'

'You're ill, and not fit to be left,' explained Phil, as he looked at him very thoughtfully.

'What do you know about it?'

'And I'd much rather stop—oh! so much rather, if you'll let me,' pleaded his son.

'Well—I'm blowed,' muttered Foxy Wharton.

He lay and considered this proposition, staring hard at Phil until a fresh shivering fit seized him, and his great white teeth rattled like castanets.

'Go—why don't you go? Every one of you,' he screamed at last, 'don't you see the money

we're chucking away?   Phil, you won't run off
and leave us?'

'No—not now.'

'Say, "wish you may die, if you do."'

Phil said it to please his suspicious parent,
but he still remained at the bedside and looked
imploringly at the others.

'Leave me with him,' he said at last, 'he is
my father, and I have a right to stop.'

'I tell you to get away,' said Mr. Wharton;
'I hate the sight of you.'

And Phil, at this paternal remark, got up and
departed with the minstrels forthwith.   But he
could not sing that day; his voice trembled and
was out of tune, and he thought in his heart he
was going to be ill like his father.

'Something's the matter with the boy,'
thought the visitors, and the absence of the
big, bland Mr. Moriega was explained to a few
inquirers who were full of sympathy. Phil
looked round once for Mr. Miles and his wife,
but, true to their new line of policy not to look
conspicuous and arouse fresh suspicions, they
were not upon the sands, and presently, and

before the entertainment was over, Phil slipped away and went back to the little cottage near the pier.

Here he found his father much worse, and a neighbour from next door attending upon him, and endeavouring to pacify him. At sight of Phil he was a little calmer, and the ruling passion was strong in him for a moment again.

'What's the take this morning?' he inquired, hoarsely.

'Three pounds odd.'

'Where's the money?' he asked; 'who's got the money?'

'Biggins.'

'Biggins is a thief, and will stick to the lot if we don't look after him.'

'I don't think he will.'

'You did not run away, then,' he said, after a long pause.

'No.'

'Why didn't you?'

'I—I couldn't leave you like this,' replied Phil, in a low voice.

'Why not?'

'I may go when you are strong and well again, but I shouldn't like to slip off to-day,' said Phil, thoughtfully. 'I don't know why, except it seems so strange to leave you now.'

Foxy Wharton glared at his son, and tried to speak again—this time failing and making a miserable noise instead. Phil ran out of the house, and on his own responsibility went in search of a doctor, whom he brought back with him, and who pronounced Mr. Wharton, *alias* Moriega, in a very bad way indeed, although extremely guarded in his opinion as to what was the matter with the gentleman.

He recommended perfect quiet, and the withdrawal of the minstrels to another lodging, and Foxy Wharton was too ill to utter anything by way of protest. He could just stretch his hand out towards his son, and say, in a sad, piteous tone, 'Don't go away, Phil,' and that was his last coherent phrase for a considerable period of time. He was raving with brain-fever before the day was over, and the news took an exaggerated shape, as news will, now and then, and the worthy souls of Tenby were scared the next morning by the news that scarlet fever or small-pox, or scarlet fever *and* small-pox combined, had seized upon the 'Minstrels of the Tyrol,' and heaven and the doctor only knew how many of them were down in it. This alarming news was circulated in the market-place on Saturday, and detailed over shop-counters and at street corners, the result being that when the 'Minstrels of the Tyrol,' *minus* the Moriegas, father and son, appeared upon the sands, there was a general stampede away from them, and they were left to two empty bathing-machines, a blind man, and a dog with a tin mug in his mouth.

There was a hurried consultation as to ways and means, and by the afternoon train the minstrels hurried away to Milford, and were fiddling and singing in the streets that evening with but indifferent success. They would have taken Phil away with them, but he refused to go, and was deaf to all entreaties, threats, or promises. The law was very clearly on his side now, and, as the members of the company did not see well how to break it with impunity,

they hastened away and were seen no more in
Tenby. Were seen never again, we may add,
by Philip Wharton or his father.

CHAPTER XI.

' IN GOOD HANDS.'

MANY days passed before Mr. Wharton, better
known to the Welsh folk as Moriega, was conscious enough to become aware that his band
of singers and players had vanished away from
him. When he came back to himself, or to his
senses, he was very strangely weak; and life
lay before him very strangely too, like a steep
up-hill track over a foggy moorland, and in
crossing which rugged way, so weak and faint
as he was, the odds were that he would die.

Phil thought he would die, though he had
never faced death before, or known anything of
the signs and shadows of it; the neighbours,
sympathetic in their rough, homely fashion,

were sure Mr. Moriega was not long for this world; the doctor, in his heart of hearts, had not any hope of him. The fever had burned itself out, but it had burned away the life of the man too, and here was almost the end of it, unless signs and tokens, neighbours' prophecies and doctor's forebodings, were all equally delusive.

The first sign of his better estate in one respect was in his recognition of Phil sitting by his bedside watching him attentively, with his thin hands upon his knees.

'Have you been there long?' he asked, in a faint whisper.

'Not very long,' was the reply.

'Since the morning when I was taken ill?' he asked again.

'Off and on—yes.'

'For how long now?'

'Ten days or more.'

'Good lor', you don't say so!' .

Then he put his hand up with a great effort to his head, which he found as smooth and shiny as a billiard ball. This was a new surprise, and not having struggled out of his delirium a perfect Christian, as people always do in very proper books, he took a long breath for a good swear, and got through most of it before he gave over suddenly.

'Don't go on like that now, father,' cried Phil.

'Because—why?'

'Because you mustn't.'

'Oh! mustn't I? We'll see about—who the blazes has been and shaved my head?' he asked, indignantly, but very faintly still.

'The doctor.'

'I'll about kill him when I get round,' he muttered, 'see if I don't, the brute. What business——'

And then Mr. Wharton had to give up, being entirely pumped out of breath for that occasion.

'You are to keep very quiet, father,' said Phil, 'and to be kept very quiet.'

Mr. Wharton did not answer. He lay and looked at his son steadily until his eyes closed by degrees, and he passed away again into dreamland.

Later on in the night he mustered up strength to feel his head very carefully again, as if exceedingly perplexed by its smoothness and spherical conformation, and to mutter,

'He'll pay for his larks presently. A pretty game to be up to when a fellow couldn't help himself. Phil!'

'Yes, father.'

'Where are they all?'

'Gone.'

'Run away? The lot of them?'

Phil nodded.

'Why didn't you?'

Phil did not reply to this.

'They asked you?'

Phil nodded again.

'Ah! I think I see,' were the last words he said that night.

But in the morning he saw more than that, as men sick unto death do see at times, when the great Hand draws the curtain aside. The doctor came, and told him, after Phil had been sent away upon some errand, all that Phil had done to nurse and watch him, and help those who nursed and watched along with him; he spoke of the unselfishness, even of the affection of the boy, distressed and amazed at this man of mighty strength and force reduced to such a strait as this.

'Do you think he's sorry, then?' asked the sick man, wonderingly.

'I'm sure he is.'

'It's not likely. About as sorry as you are for making me this infernal scarecrow of a Chinaman. What did you go and——'

'There, there, you must take things very calmly, Mr. Moriega. You must not excite yourself in the least,' said the doctor, laying his hand gently on the shoulder of his patient.

'How would you like *your* ugly head shaved?' muttered Wharton.

'I should be glad, if it gave me a better chance of life,' was the ready answer.

Foxy Wharton considered this; then he said, very sharply,

'Has it given me any chance?'

'It was necessary. It——'

' Look here.   Am I going to pull through, or to die?'

' That is in God's hands, not mine.'

' What do *you* think?'

A doctor does not care to be pressed for a definite opinion as to the condition of his patient, but the man seemed anxious to know the exact truth, and there might be reasons why he should.

' I am afraid, my poor fellow,' he said, after another moment's hesitation, ' that you will not get over this.'

' You know I sha'n't.'

' No, I don't know,' said the doctor.

Foxy Wharton did not ask any more questions; did not say much during the rest of the day—only towards evening he made a sign, to which the watchful Phil at once responded.

' You want me, father.   What is it?'

' Ask that—organist chap—to come and see me,' he whispered.   ' Look alive—I'm getting precious—weak.'

Phil gave a frightened look at him, and darted away.   Half-an-hour afterwards, he and Folkestone Miles, and a third figure, who stood in the background, were in the room together.

'Who else have you brought with—you?' the weak man asked, feebly.

'A minister,' said Phil. 'Mr. Miles thought you would like to see him presently.'

'I—don't want any minister,' he answered, with a hard laugh. 'What next?'

'Shall I send him away? Ask him to come to-morrow? Tell him——'

'No. *Let him be*,' muttered Wharton; then he turned to Folkestone Miles, who was looking at him through his glasses very curiously.

'You've been a friend to Phil,' he said; 'do you mind—my saying—thankee?'

'I am glad to have your thanks.'

'He has—a wonderful—voice. Look after him, will you?'

'I will,' was the promise given here.

'Thankee again. He's been in bad hands— but it hasn't—spoilt the boy.'

'No.'

A smile—a very strange smile—lighted up the broad, white face for an instant, as he whispered, very faintly,

'In good—hands—now!'

Philip Wharton is a great singer at the present time—a rich man, it is said, and one who makes good use of his riches, and turns not his back upon old friends; takes trouble even, people say, to find out old friends and help them in his way, as they helped him, in old times, in theirs. There are a few who set him down as a trifle too eccentric even for a popular professional. He is bringing out an oratorio, in which a Mr. Folkestone Miles is deeply interested, and which Francis Poofer, a musical critic of light and leading, and who writes oratorios himself, says will fail, let Wharton try all he may to force it down the throats of the public, and take the principal tenor part in it, and all that nonsense. But Philip Wharton says it shall succeed, and slaps the back of Mr. Miles,—who is his sole and permanent accompanyist at all the concerts, and who is doing very well indeed—and adds that he means it to be the big hit of the season.

Yes—an eccentric man, Mr. Wharton. He

walks all the way to the Westminster Bridge Road to have his hair cut at Broadbrook's 'Hair Cutting Saloon and Fashionable Emporium '— an establishment all plate-glass front, wax dummies, and ivory hair-brushes—and how Mr. Broadbrook managed to start such a business as that, all of a sudden too, no one in Lambeth, aware of Mr. Broadbrook's antecedents, has ever been able to make out.

Phil Wharton knows, and Folkestone Miles can make a very tolerable guess.

MR. BIRD'S BEST UMBRELLA.

MR. BIRD'S BEST UMBRELLA.

' RAT-A-TAT-A-TAT-A-TAT-A-TAT-A-TAT—BANG !
There was a pause, and a long enough pause to
give me the impression that I had been dreaming of earthquakes, or of the bombardment of
the British Museum, or of a volcanic eruption in
Russell Square, to convince me even forcibly
that I *must* have been dreaming, as I sat up in
bed, and rubbed my eyes and listened. Then
—Bang! bang! bang!—rat-a-tat-a-tat-a-tat-a-
tat-a-tat-a-tat—Bang! Yes, there was somebody evidently knocking at the street-door,
hanging by the street-door knocker, and throw-
ing his whole soul into the instrument—the
house was on fire perhaps, or we were wanted

next door at Brian's, or a lunatic had escaped, and was clamouring for admittance, strait-waistcoat and all, or else the upstairs lodgers had come back prematurely from their visit to Tunbridge, and were anxious to get in out of the rain, which was coming down with a vehemence that was certainly startling. I could surmise nothing more at a moment's notice and at half-past two in the morning.

We all slept very soundly in No. 10, Prossiter Street, Prossiter Place, Russell Square, Bloomsbury, for we worked very hard at No. 10, and the house was a large one. It was a house of many lodgers—parlour-floor, first-floor, and second-floor—and all comfortably let, and those lodgers who were at home were all fast asleep, or else waiting for me, the poor, weakly proprietor of the establishment (Jane Neild, at your service, gentle reader, age twenty-two, and an orphan with an establishment on her mind, and a living to get out of the establishment), to call to the servants (Bridget, able-bodied, 'general,' aged forty, and a frightful temper, and Sarah, aged thirteen, child with a chronic cold and a red nose, but handy as a help to Bridget) to get up and see what was the matter at No. 10, or with the party outside No. 10 who was 'kicking up such a deuce of a row.'

That was the way it was put at last by Captain Choppers, my drawing-room floor, an irritable old gentleman—not to say violent when roused—who came out on the landing at last in an attire which Bridget told me afterwards was far from decorous, and began bawling vociferously up the staircase the names of each of my maids in turn, concluding with my own name in a shriek of sheer despair.

'Miss Neild—here, I say—is everybody dead? Miss N-e-e-e-ild!'

'Bless my soul, captain, what is it now?' I cried, through the crack in my door.

'Don't you hear that infernal noise downstairs, madam? Who the deuce is it at this time of night, who the—*what* do you say, madam?'

'I'm going to open the window, and inquire, unless you——'

'It's no business of mine, Miss Neild,' bawled

the captain. 'I don't expect anybody—I'm not going into the drawing-room at this time of night, with my cold. I'm disturbed enough, as it is, through your being all so diabolically deaf. I shall leave this day week, ma'am. There.'

And slam went the back drawing-room door, and crick-crack went the key in the irascible captain's lock. I was in my dressing-room, with a flannel garment, which I take the liberty here of calling a 'muffler,' wrapped round my head and shoulders; and, as I went towards the window, trembling, I must say, in every limb, the knocking was repeated for the third time, and with a threefold vigour, born of the delay and irritation at the gross want of attention to past summonses.

I waited till there was silence again, or nearly silence—for I could distinctly hear Captain Choppers loading all his firearms—and then opened the window, and peered down into the damp, shiny street, which the wind and rain had all to themselves, with the exception of a dark figure on my top step, whose hat, I could see, was as shiny as the pavement.

'What is it?' I inquired; but the wind whisked my voice into Museum Street, and I had to repeat the inquiry in a shrill falsetto. The man below paused with his hand to the knocker again—for he was just going to begin afresh—listened, and then ran down the steps and stood on the edge of the kerbstone, with his hands behind him, looking up at me at last. I could make nothing of him in the darkness from my point of view.

'What do you want, sir?' I asked, now that I had secured the attention of this individual. 'What are you making such a noise for, at this time of night?'

'I'm very sorry to disturb you, lady——'

'So it seems,' I said, acrimoniously; but he did not hear me, and perhaps it was as well he did not. I have not a reputation for being severe in my remarks, but then this was an exceptional proceeding, and deserved rebuke.

'The fact is, madam, the wind has blown my umbrella clean out of my hand into your area. I would not mind so much,' he condescended to explain still further, at the top of his voice, 'but

it's an umbrella I set great store by.   Besides,
it's raining tremendously.'

'I really cannot come down at this hour and
get your umbrella,' I said, severely; 'you must
call to-morrow for it.'

'Isn't there anyone in the house—any man—
who can get it?'

'The house is locked up for the night.'

'It's such a very deep area, or I would drop
over and get it myself—but then I don't see
how to get out again,' he said.

'I can't help you, sir; I am very sorry,' I
replied, 'but I can't go down to-night for it.'

'I should be a brute to ask you, ma'am,' he
said, politely now; and here I could see he
raised his hat to me; 'of course I could not tell
who was in the house, or whether it might not
be easy to get my umbrella—which I really
value very much, I assure you; it's an umbrella
which—but I am very sorry to have disturbed
you.   I will call in the morning—thank you,
good-night.'

And away the gentleman strode, turning up
the collar of his coat above his ears as he went

on down the street. I closed the window, I set my 'muffler' aside, and in another moment I should have been in my humble couch again, when Rat-a-tat-a-tat-a-tat-a-tat-a-tat-a-tat-a-tat —Bang! once more aroused the echoes of the neighbourhood, but brought no policeman to the rescue, or any anxious inquirers to the windows, except myself, who, once more en-wrapped, and this time trembling with indig-nation, was a minute afterwards in my old position facing the dangers and inconveniences of the gale, and looking down once more at the figure below me, standing in his old position on the brink of the deep gutter in the roadway.

'I beg your pardon again very much, I am awfully sorry to be such a nuisance, but I really don't know where I am,' he cried, rattling on with great volubility. 'I haven't the least idea, and the streets are all alike, and I am quite a stranger to this part of the world, and I am afraid I sha'n't know this house from any other in the daylight. Might I just trouble you for the address?'

'Prossiter Street,' I called down to him.

' I thank you very much. Boshington Street.'

' Prossiter Street,' I screamed.

' Prossiter—a thousand thanks and apologies. And what number, ma'am, may I ask ?'

' No. 10.'

' I am very much obliged to you,' he bawled forth, ' I am exceedingly indebted ; I would not have troubled you in this way if the umbrella had not been——'

But I would not listen to any further explanation ; he had already said that he set great store by the umbrella, and I did not want to hear that fact again with the rain coming down like a waterspout, and the wind blowing every way at once. I closed the window summarily and cut short his volubility, and the instant afterwards I heard him running along towards New Oxford Street as if to make up for lost time, or to overtake a passing cab of which he had probably caught sight.

It was some time before I could get to sleep after so lengthy a discussion under such peculiar circumstances. I was annoyed at the man's pertinacity concerning his trumpery umbrella, his indifference to time, and the personal inconvenience to which he exposed people by his unseasonable request, and I lay in considerable fear of his third return and another series of questions at the top of his lungs. But he came not again, and I dropped off to sleep at last, and was troubled by dreams of tempests, and tornadoes, and white squalls carrying away whole grosses of umbrellas, till Sarah knocked at the panels of my door with her customary information that it was half-past six o'clock.

I was perforce an early riser. There was a great deal to superintend, and my parlour-floor was a gentleman connected with the railway goods traffic department, who was always getting up early and going out to business and letting himself in again with his latch-key about seven in the morning, when he expected breakfast ready, and ate it walking about the room, as a rule, preparatory to running away again in hot haste. I should have considered Mr. Goode an irritable lodger if it had not been for the angelic contrast that he afforded to Captain Choppers. As it was, he seemed only a little bit fussy and precise, which was attributable chiefly to his lot in life. Mr. Goode was a widower with two sons at boarding-school, and if those boys had lived and died at boarding-school, instead of coming home twice a year for the holidays, I think Bridget and Sarah would have rejoiced exceedingly.

I remember Mr. Goode asked Sarah that morning if he could speak with Miss Neild before he left, and I went upstairs at once to see him.   He was walking about with his mouth full and a slice of bread-and butter in his hand.

'That was a dreadful noise last night, Miss Neild,' he began; 'I couldn't get a wink of sleep.   The captain, I suppose, again?   I must certainly ask you in my name to present my compliments to him, and——'

'It was not Captain Choppers.'

'Indeed.   No.   Well, I thought I heard his voice,' said Mr. Goode, very much disappointed.

There was no homogeneousness between Mr. Goode and Captain Choppers—I may say even that there were times when they hated and loathed each other.

'He's a beggarly upstart civilian, madam,' the captain would roar in excited moments; and 'He a captain!' Mr. Goode would say with withering contempt. 'Captain of a penny steamboat, perhaps, nothing more.'

But to my strange story.

'A gentleman dropped his umbrella down the area and knocked me up for it,' I explained, with a little acrimonious emphasis.

'Well, of all the confounded impertinence!' exclaimed Mr. Goode; 'I should like to treat that party to a bit of my mind. You never got up and gave it to him.'

'No, I did not.'

'I am glad to hear that. For you must take care of yourself, Miss Neild, and keep strong. You are not looking well,' he said, regarding me with his head on one side as if he had a troublesome wen on the other which he was anxious to keep clear of the edge of his shirt-collar, 'upon my word you are not. You are pale and fragile-looking. A little change at the seaside now would do you a world of good.'

'Yes, I daresay it would.'

'This large house is a trial to you—and that captain, with his absurd fancies and his ridiculous tempers, would worry the life out of a saint —and you are really looking extremely pale this morning. And—good gracious I had no idea it was so late !'

Mr. Goode swallowed the last portion of his bread-and-butter whole, and dashed like a harlequin out of the front door. When he had gone I surveyed myself in his parlour glass and wondered if I was looking very ill, or whether, being a dismal man, he was trying to frighten me, and I arrived at the conclusion I was looking about the same as usual, 'a prim, pale, pert little puss,' as my dear old dad called me once, when I was arguing with him on the house-keeping expenses, and how the weekly money would never hold out if he would continually ask the lodgers into supper and a game at cribbage afterwards.

Poor dad, he died next year, and left me sole proprietor of the lease and furniture of the house in Prossiter Street, and there were no late suppers and cribbage any more. I was seventeen when he died, and I had had five years' charge of No. 10 since—'getting quite an old maid, Lily Brian, who lived next door, said; but then Lily was four years younger than I, and assumed upon her youth, as girls will. A nice girl was Lily Brian, and my one friend and confidante, but perhaps too fond of laughing at everything, although that showed she was happy and had a keen sense of humour and a fine set of teeth.

Well, perhaps I *was* a trifle paler, was my second conclusion after the first five minutes, and with a tinge of redness—a mere tinge—about the nose, just as if I was 'breeding a cold,' as Bridget put it. And this was not remarkable, considering last night's experiences, and sure enough the cold *was* bred before my early dinner-hour, when the sneezing stage had set in with considerable force. This reminded me once more of the umbrella which had been dropped into the area last night, and I asked Bridget to bring it to me.

'The what, m'm?' asked Bridget, with a wild stare.

'The umbrella.'

'Umbereller, and down our airy, did ye say, m'm? There's not a scrap of umbereller down our airy. I've been in and out twenty toimes, and must have seen it,' continued Bridget.

'Bridget, there *must* be an umbrella,' I said, 'go and see.'

Bridget departed and returned with the information that there was no umbrella in the area, and then I went and looked for myself, and, as it was still drizzling with rain, I caught another cold on the top of the first one, and was at fever heat ere twenty-four hours had ensued. But before then the gentleman had called for his property, and I had met face to face the individual who had rendered last night hideous.

He came at three in the afternoon, sending in his card by way of preliminary announcement that he had arrived. I did not associate him with the umbrella—indeed, I was feeling drowsy and 'out of sorts,' with pains at the back of my head, when a huge glazed card was presented to me bearing the inscription in large fancy letters of 'GEOFFRY BIRD, Carver and Gilder and Picture-Frame Maker, 967, Goswell Road, Islington, N.'

'I don't want any picture-frames, Sarah,' I said to my small help, wearily.

'It's the gentleman about his umbrella, mum,' said Sarah.

'Good Heavens! Oh, indeed. Well, ask him to step in, then.'

My sitting-room was a small apartment at the end of the long passage, the only little room I had to myself and my day-dreams—yes, my day-dreams!—when the house was full, which it had been all these years, for they were the same lodgers who had lived with us in father's time—odd, inconsiderate, queer-tempered lodgers enough, but faithful to my house, and keeping an old promise to my father, too, 'to stand by the little woman a bit when he was gone.'

Mr. Bird was ushered into my presence, and he came in with a low bow and with a trifle too much of a smile to wholly please me, although it suggested itself to me somewhat quaintly that he would not have much to smile at presently. Mr. Bird was a slim and somewhat short young man who wore his black hair long enough for a violinist, and had upon the smallest of hands the reddest and most prominent of knuckles. He was rather a good-looking young man, with brown eyes and black bushy eyebrows, and with a habit of shaking his head suddenly, as if to get the hair back from his forehead, or as if he had just come up out of water. He was fairly well dressed, might have passed even for a gentleman if it had not been for his red knuckles and that very obtrusive smile.

'Good afternoon, Miss Neild—for I understand your name *is* Neild,' he began; 'I am very sorry for the third time in my life to be such a complete nuisance to you. But I think I am in the right this time, being here by invitation.'

'Yes; I asked you to call at a more seasonable hour, I remember,' I replied, 'but——'

'And I owe you no end of apologies,' he added, 'for the noise I made last night. I was in too much of a hurry—I am naturally impulsive, in fact—and when the wind caught my umbrella, and blew it clean out of my hands into your area, my first impulse was to run up the steps and knock.'

'Yes, I heard you knock,' I said, quietly.

'No, I'm sure you didn't,' he said, flatly contradicting me here; 'you couldn't have heard me the first time, for I waited a reasonable period before I knocked again. It was a tremendous while to wait with a fellow drenched to the skin all the time. By George, I was never out in such a rain. I shall catch a nice cold, I am afraid. You have a bad cold, young lady?'

'I caught cold last night.'

'Not—not at *that* window?'

'Yes, at that window.'

'Oh, come, I am awfully sorry for that,' Mr. Bird cried, 'I didn't think of that. I thought some gentleman, or servant, or porter might be up, for there was a light burning over the hall door, and it wouldn't be a great deal of trouble and save my getting wet through. Why, I would much rather have lost my umbrella altogether than have given *you* cold, although it's an umbrella which I would not take twenty pounds for —no, nor fifty pounds either.'

'Is it a very valuable umbrella?'

'Oh no, not at all; but, as you know now, it's my best umbrella in every sense of the word,' he said, laughing, 'my very best umbrella, don't you see?'

But I did not see; neither the application nor the umbrella was apparent to me, and my heart quite sank at the news which I had to impart to him. The man was so enwrapped in his umbrella—speaking figuratively—that I felt it was necessary to break the news gently.

'I'm sorry to say I don't see,' I replied, 'for the fact is——'

Yes, he was impulsive, and dashed to conclusions; and the smile *did* leave his face as suddenly and completely as if somebody had pulled it away by a string, and a settled look of horror, and for an instant open-mouthed idiocy, took its place.

'The fact is——' he repeated, very slowly at last; 'go on, please.'

'That there was no umbrella down our area at all.'

'Oh! that won't do,' he exclaimed, so abruptly and rudely that I felt the colour coming up all over me, 'that won't do at any price.'

'I don't know what you mean by any price, sir,' I said, drawing myself up to my full height, as the novelists say—and that height was exactly five feet three inches and a half when fully drawn and a little bit on tiptoe—'but you must take my word, sir, that I haven't set eyes on your umbrella.'

'No, Miss Neild, I don't suppose you have,' he said, very quickly; 'don't think that I think that you think—that—that—why, of course I don't,' he said, tumbling into another sentence as the first one became hopelessly involved, 'and it's not at all likely; but it went down your area—I was perfectly sober—and the servants must have seen it in the morning. May I ask the servants?'

'I have asked them.'

'Isn't there a page-boy, or somebody who comes early to clean something?'

'No.'

'Who is the first to go into that area in the

morning, Miss Neild?' he inquired—' somebody for coals, I suppose?'

' Bridget or Sarah, certainly.'

' I should very much like to see Bridget and Sarah,' he suggested, ' if you would not object.'

' You must be content with my word, sir, that your umbrella is not on the premises,' I said, still loftily ; ' I cannot have my servants subjected to a cross-examination on this question. I have already made every inquiry.'

' And they tell you they have not seen my umbrella?'

' They do.'

' And you believe them?'

' Certainly.'

' Well, I don't—and that's plain speaking,' he said, frankly.

' I'm aware of that.'

' Because, you see, it is quite impossible, unless there's anybody else in the house who gets up earlier than the servants. Is there anybody else?' he asked.

' Yes, there's a gentleman who lodges in my front parlours, who leaves very early, but——'

'That's the man. Where is he?' cried Mr. Bird, with a frantic dash in a new direction of suspicion, 'I should like to see him.'

'He's a gentleman holding a high position on the railway, and is not at all likely to confiscate property that does not belong to him,' I said.

'I don't say he has confiscated it,' answered Mr. Bird, less brusquely, 'but he may have seen it this morning, and put it aside for further inquiries.'

'Mr. Goode is not in the habit of going into my area,' I said; 'I don't believe he has been in the area in the whole course of his life.'

'Not before this morning, Miss Neild—very likely not, having nothing to go for, as it were. But when he caught sight of an umbrella—and a very peculiar umbrella—lying on the wet stones, I haven't the slightest doubt——'

'He could not get into the area, sir,' I said; 'Bridget takes up the key with her every night, and, besides, I told him about the umbrella this morning.'

'What did he say to that?'

'He said it was like your impertinence—

"confounded impertinence," I may say were the actual words used,' I answered; 'to make such a noise in the middle of the night, and he should like to give you a piece of his mind.'

'Oh! he said that, did he?' he remarked, biting his finger-nails almost savagely.

'Yes.'

'Then he's the man who's got my umbrella,' he cried; 'I see it all now. He's keeping it back out of spite!'

'Mr. Bird, this is absolutely unendurable.'

'I suppose he was the fellow bellowing about the house like a bull last night, trying to make somebody understand that I was knocking. I heard him.'

'No, he was not the *fellow*,' I replied, severely; 'that was Captain Choppers.'

'Does Captain Choppers get up early?'

'No, he doesn't, he's a very late riser indeed; I believe he's in bed now.'

'That's his artfulness,' said the suspicious individual, 'just to make you fancy——'

But I could not allow him to proceed any further. I was fairly roused by this stranger's disparaging reflections. I rose, looked steadily and gravely at him, and said—

'This interview is at an end, Mr. Bird. These gentlemen are my lodgers—I might say almost my friends—and I cannot listen to your cruel and uncalled-for remarks against their common honesty.'

'Common honesty it may be, Miss Neild,' he replied; 'but you must allow there is very uncommon dishonesty somewhere in your establishment.'

'I will allow nothing.'

'I don't mean I want you to allow me anything for the loss of my umbrella,' he said, hurriedly. 'Pray don't understand that to be my wish.'

'Of course not. The idea!'

'That's all right then; very likely I am a little put out—rude, in fact,' he added, apologetically, 'for I'm not a lady's man, and don't know anything about ladies; but, as I am quite prepared to take my oath the umbrella *did* go down your area, it's rather aggravating to be told you don't believe a word I say.'

'I never said that,' I answered.

'I shall find it all out my own way, I daresay; I have got a habit of sifting to the bottom of things, they tell me—but I will not trouble you any more about it, Miss Neild. If I have been a bit rough,' he said, 'I'll ask you to forgive me, and to believe I don't think for an instant *you* know anything about it. Heaven forbid, with such a nice look as you've got——'

'Sir!'

'I beg pardon. Don't mind me; I'm bothered,' he ran on, with extraordinary volubility, 'and this umbrella was my old father's last present—just three days before he died—when he was given up, and one would have thought he had had something more serious to consider than buying me an umbrella for my birthday. He died on my birthday, too, which is another odd part of the story,' he ran on; 'but there, good-day, madam, I am bothering you. I wish your cold better—good-day.'

And away marched Mr. Geoffry Bird out of my room, and down the long passage to the street-door, swinging his arms wildly to and fro. He jumped the whole flight of steps into the street, and was gone, as I thought, for good.

The next day I was very ill indeed—too ill to rise. I had caught cold at the open window and in the damp night air, and it had become absolutely necessary to send for the doctor, and to make what I always considered was too much of a fuss over me. Lily Brian told me a week afterwards, when I was able to sit up for the first time in my room, that I had been in a critical state, and there had been one night when everybody was anxious and excited, and even Captain Choppers walked continuously up and down the stairs for two hours and a half, and said, 'Poor girl, poor girl,' and had a secret conference with Mr. Goode as to the advisability of having a physician in the morning, at their mutual expense, and 'say nothing about it, sir, to anyone.' But I was better that next morning: I changed for the better with the summer weather which came in, bright, and fine, and hot, and suggested holidays out of town and by the great green sea for the lucky folk who could afford to spend their money.

Lily Brian and her mother and father, and two gawky brothers whom I did not like very much, and thirteen small members of the family, were all going out of town, and 'Why not come with us?' Lily had said, kindly.

My answer was a very old one, and very natural, and very truthful too.

'Because I cannot afford it, Lily.'

'Oh, bother the money,' said Lily.

'That's what I often say myself.'

'It shall cost you next to nothing—hardly anything,' Lily suggested. 'Papa says you will only have to pay for a room somewhere, and you can board with us, and oh, dear, it will be awfully jolly!'

'It's very kind of your papa, and—and I'll think of it, Lily, at any rate.'

'And make up your mind and say "yes,"' cried Lily—'won't you, Jane?'

'I don't know.'

'That fright of a captain's going somewhere, I know,' Lily said, 'and Mr. Goode has got a free pass down the line, you tell me, and he's sure to go into the country with so little to pay for it : it's just like him. And do think of it, Jane, there's a love!'

I did think of it. Thought of Mr. Brian's large family, eighteen of them altogether, and whether it was possible I could intrude gracefully upon them. Mr. Brian had retired from a cocoa-nut fibre and street-door mat business in the Tottenham Court Road, and was pretty well off, with only a slight necessity for letting his drawing-room floor. He was evidently not a rich man, and there were a few struggles to 'keep up an appearance,' although he went out of town with his family for a month every summer, by express desire of Mrs. Brian, who required change every August, and regularly sallied forth, *en famille*, from her large establishment in Prossiter Street to a house down a back slum in High Street, Margate, where the rooms were small, and the children were heaped together sardine fashion, and now and then came back with 'something catching,' as a wind-up to the season's enjoyment.

And this particular August I was asked to

join them. There was the sea, and 'You must take a little change,' said the doctor, and Lily Brian was very pressing, and Captain Choppers had talked of going away for a week or two, and the boys Goode were coming home for the holidays, and I, Jane Neild, was able to pay—and would insist upon paying—my fair share for board with the Brians, having my little room out of the house, too, for that peace and quietness which is not always found in large families. Yes, I would go down to Margate when I was strong—when I was well enough to bear the fatigue of the journey.

This was a promise on the day the Brians, with much formality of departure, left town for the season, and I made up my mind to get well and strong as soon as possible, and join them. When I was downstairs again in my little back room there was a great surprise awaiting me. Nailed against the wall, under my father's cabinet-sized photograph, was a brand-new ornament—a little carving in oak of a dead bird hanging by its claws head downwards, and with every feather wonderfully delineated. I stared at it with intense astonishment, and Bridget stood in the background with a grin on her face from ear to ear.

'Where did this come from? Good gracious, how beautiful! how—well, I never did!'

My thoughts flashed to Mr. Goode, for he was liberal at times, and grateful for any little attentions in his widowerhood's estate in the shape of darning socks or re-establishing the security of buttons; but the truth soon came out, and then I was more astonished than ever.

'If you please, m'm, it's the young man who lost his umbereller,' explained Bridget, with a loud guffaw at last and a violent stamping of both her big Irish feet, like an excitable person with a bone in her throat.

'What!'

'Yes, m'm,' continued Bridget; 'and I was to say nothing about it to anybody but you— and not till you were downstairs again—because he wouldn't have you worried about anything, he said, not for worlds.'

'He said all that?'

'Yes, m'm.'

'But, bless the man,' I exclaimed, 'what has he left this here for?'

'It's—it's a prisent, m'm, I'm thinking.'

'A present to me, and from that impertinent being!' I said; 'I'll see about his present presently.   When did he come?'

'He's been here every day, m'm.'

'Every day?'

'Twice a day,' Bridget replied. 'And the day you were so ill he came three times, to make sure the doctors weren't killing you.'

'It's very extraordinary.'

'He *is* 'stronary, m'm,' asserted Bridget, 'shure, and there's not much doubt of it. The way he axed me and badgered me about that umbereller, m'm, every day after you were took ill, you'd have thought he was a judge and jury rolled into one—and Sarah, too, poor critter.'

'I never heard of such behaviour in my life.'

'Right ye are, Miss Neild, as far as that goes; but when Sarah bust out crying at last he was very sorry and gave her 'arf-a-crown; and so he did me, m'm, like a real gentleman, when I thought it was quite time I cried too, when 'arf-crowns were flying about like that.'

'That'll do, Bridget,' I said—for Bridget when loquacious was familiar—'when was he here last?'

'This morning.'

'Indeed.'

'And I told him you were quite come round, and he said, "That's a good job," and went away.'

'Do you think he'll return?'

'I don't think so, m'm, for he said, "Good-bye, Bridget; mind you take care of her," as he walked hisself off.'

'Did he say anything else?'

'N—no, m'm, I don't seem to recollect——'

'Answer me truthfully, Bridget; what else did he say?'

'Sorra a word else, except he hoped Margate would do you a power of good.'

'How did he know I was going to Margate?' I inquired.

'That's more nor mortal can say, m'm. He knows a great deal more about other people's affairs than he ought. He interferes like, doesn't he?   He's a terrible curious young man.'

'Bridget, you *have* something more to tell me, I'm sure you have.'

'Oh ! Miss Neild.'

'How dare you deceive me ! how dare——'

'Mercy on us, my dear mistress, don't go and throw yourself all the way back agin by flaring off like this.   I'll tell ye everything, and it's not much, after all, if ye'll only keep cool and comfor'ble.'

'Well--go on.'

'And ye may give me a month's warning and send me away arterwards, if ye'll only be cool, Miss, and don't blame me too much jest at prisint.'

'Why don't you explain?'

'Well, then, he took it into his head Mr. Goode had got his umbereller or else Captain Choppers, and one day, when they were both out, he axed me to let him look into their rooms, and I did, m'm—and begorra I shouldn't have been surprised if either of 'em *had* got it, mane souls that they are, with never a kind word to those who are slaving their hearts out for 'em, and——'

'Bridget, go downstairs directly.'

'To be sure, m'm, I will if ye don't want me any more.'

Bridget departed, and it dawned upon me that she had been imbibing just a little—and this had occurred once before, when papa was alive. And she had too, but it was for joy that I was better, and to drink good luck to me, she afterwards confessed, and I forgave her, especially as on the next day she joined the Blue Ribbon movement, in sheer contriteness of spirit, and was for ever afterwards—that is, up till now —a worthy, if humble, member of society.

But this Mr. Geoffry Bird, how the man did trouble me! How his nasty suspicious nature had led him to poke and pry about my establishment, and to take advantage of my helplessness, and the proneness of Bridget and Sarah for half-crowns, to ransack the whole place! My blood boiled with indignation. And then his present! —if it were a present—obtrusively nailed against the wall, too, as if *I* cared for his carvings, or did anything but despise his miserable manners and his uncharitable self. He could not take my word that no one had stolen his umbrella, oh, dear no! He must prove for himself that I was not speaking the truth. How I hated him!

I was recommended to take a drive next day, and I hired a hansom cab and went to Goswell Road, Islington, with the carved bird. I discovered No. 967 at last, and found the house empty, and a bill with 'THIS HOUSE TO LET' pasted upon the shutters. Mr. Geoffry Bird had left the neighbourhood within the last few days, and no one in Goswell Road knew what had become of him.

So I had my journey for nothing, and all the expenses of payment for carrying me through the heart of the big city, where there was not a breath of air stirring that hot day. I do not think the drive did me any good, I was so terribly vexed that Mr. Bird was not to be discovered, and that I had to return to Prossiter Street with his hateful carving on my lap. I would have thrown it out of the cab only I was afraid of hitting somebody between the eyes and creating an uproar in the metropolis.

'Put that wretched thing away where I can't see it,' I said to Bridget, on my return.

'Yes, m'm, leave it to me, m'm.'

'I don't mean where we can't find it,' I added, meeting a decisive expression in Bridget O'Gowan's green eyes that alarmed me; 'the man *may* call again, although I doubt it very much.'

Next week I was strong enough to join the Brians at Margate—that salubrious retreat where one meets everybody he knows, if he only waits long enough. And on the jetty extension that evening I met Captain Choppers and Mr. Goode, who had both come down ' by accident,' and who had been passing each other on the jetty all the evening as though they had never met in the whole course of their lives. Mr. Goode's two sons were in Margate also, but, having fallen headlong into the water whilst fishing, had gone home to bed whilst their suits were being dried. And the next morning whom should I meet face to face, and smiling as vigorously as ever, but Geoffry Bird the carver.

It was early morning, when few people were stirring, and I had gone for a walk along the Fort to put my blood in circulation and get an appetite for breakfast. The Brians were not early risers, and I knew it was no use calling at their apartments till half-past eight o'clock.

Mr. Bird was clad in a dark blue pilot suit, with a very yellow straw hat set on the back of his head and a large telescope under his arm. He was supremely nautical, and I took him for somebody rather high in the coastguard service—a sergeant or something—before he raised his hat and came with an antelope kind of spring towards me.

'Miss Neild,' he exclaimed, 'I am so very glad to see you about again. You really cannot imagine how glad I am!'

'I don't understand why it should occasion you any pleasure, sir,' I said, in my most reserved tone of voice.

'Don't you, though? Oh, well, I'll tell you.'

He turned and walked by my side, and I did not see on the instant how it was possible to get rid of him. I felt my equanimity was seriously disturbed by his appearance, by his insufferable obtrusiveness. This was part and parcel of his ordinary behaviour—a total want of forethought, which was as evident that day as in the small hours of the morning when he had roused me out of my first sleep by nearly battering the house down.

He alluded to that little incident at once.

'In answering me that unlucky night, Miss Neild, you nearly caught your death,' he explained, 'and nobody can imagine how miserable I was—how desperately wretched—until I heard you were out of danger. I should have never forgiven myself, upon my honour, and I did not know a moment's peace till Bridget, your girl, told me you were out of danger. Lor', what a trial it was!'

'I don't see why—I don't understand at all— I——'

'I can just fancy how a man feels who has committed a murder and is not found out yet,' he continued : 'it was dreadful, and all my own fault too—every scrap of it.'

I did not feel so bitterly towards him after this. His manner was genuine, if too forcible and fluent for every-day wear. I might have even thanked him for his exaggerated interest in my health and said good-morning, if I had not suddenly remembered his surreptitious visits to my lodgers' apartments. Then I was adamant, and he saw it. He was certainly an observant man whom very little escaped. I noticed the broad smile disappear, and he said, almost with astonishment,

'Why, you're offended with me still!'

'As I have only seen you once before in my life, I cannot very well speak of being offended, Mr. Bird—but I must say——'

'No, no, don't say it,' he cried, interrupting me, 'don't say a word more, please. I—I know it was a great liberty—an unwarrantable liberty —but I couldn't help it. I wanted to make a little return for all the trouble and misery I had brought about, and I couldn't think of anything else. I had just done it, you see.'

'Done what?' I exclaimed, snappishly—I could have screamed at him for two pins.

'Why, the little bit of carving—aren't you talking about that?' he inquired.

'No, sir, although I'll trouble you to remove the article from my premises as soon as you conveniently can.'

'Oh!'

'But I am alluding now, sir, to your ungentlemanly behaviour in bribing my servants to let you inspect my apartments.'

'I didn't bribe your servants, Miss Neild. Poor girls, I frightened them, but I did not give them money as a bribe. You might have thought better of a fellow than that,' he said, very sorrowfully; 'although why you should I don't know exactly.'

'You had no right to go into my lodgers' rooms and search for that trumpery umbrella you lost.'

'No right!' he repeated.

'Certainly—no right.'

'But one of those two old beggars has got it,' he cried, energetically; 'I'm sure of that.'

'How dare you say this to me!'

'Who else can it be? I know *you* haven't got it,' he cried. 'I am sure your two servants are as innocent as babes unborn, and they were the only two besides in the house that night—the upstairs lot had gone to Tunbridge for two days.'

'How did you know that?'

'Oh, I made every inquiry,' he explained, coolly; 'and as the umbrella was a precious possession to me—I think I told you before it was a gift from my father on his dying bed—I made every effort to find out what had become of it.'

'And a very mean way to find out it was,' I said, with asperity, 'and—good-morning.'

'Go-ood morning,' he said, in a low, croaking voice. He raised his bilious straw hat, dropped his telescope, which he picked up and tucked once more under his arm, came suddenly to a full stop, and let me go on my way unmolested any further by him.

When I had got a good distance from him, I began to feel a little sorry—even a little in doubt if I had not been too hard upon him. He had appeared so utterly dumbfounded by my last opinion of his conduct, and he had turned of such a variety of colours. Perhaps, from his point of view, and with an umbrella which had vanished from every point of view, he was not wholly to be blamed. Perhaps the captain had —no, that was quite impossible. Perhaps Mr. Goode—oh! I was getting as miserably distrustful as this unhappy man.

Yes, I was a little sorry. As I went off the Fort, I stole one glance behind me to make sure what had become of him—that his impulsive nature even had not led him to jump off the cliff. He was all right, he was a long way off— indeed, in the very place where I had left him— not overwhelmed or mad with grief and shame, as I had almost feared he might be, but standing with his legs planted widely apart looking at me through his telescope. When he saw I had turned he wheeled quickly round and feigned an interest in the sea, knocking the hat off a bath-chairman just passing him with an early fare who had lost the use of his legs.

Well, there was an end of the intruder, I thought, and I could have wished—yes, I did actually wish—that I had been more of a young lady and less of a vixen in my reproaches to him. I had been put out by his appearance at Margate, by his venturing to address me, and had lost my self-composure, but then a more obtuse and aggravating person I had never encountered before.

Not so very obtuse either, but very quick to take a hint, and to guess when he was disliked and his company objected to. We passed each other twice or thrice a day after that, but he never ventured to speak to me again; he bowed with great gravity, and exhibited an extraordinary formality in taking off his hat, seizing it in the middle of the crown, and raising it like the lid off a saucepan, and there was no further occasion to object to his expansive smile. He was a stolid, even a woebegone, young man, with something on his mind. Had it not been for that everlasting telescope under his arm, one could have imagined him a prey to the deepest-rooted sorrow.

I think he was the most sad when I passed him in company with the captain, who sometimes condescended to promenade with me, and the most angry when I was out with Mr. Goode, to whom I was a relief from the wear and tear of two boys wonderfully full of animal spirits on unseasonable occasions. When I was with Lily Brian, he seemed to brighten up a little, and Lily was curious concerning him, and asked me many questions.

'Who *is* that good-looking young man, Jane, who is always taking his hat off?' she asked one morning.

'He is a carver and gilder; I don't know him —that is, I hardly know him,' I said. 'He called once about something he had dropped down our area, and he has claimed an acquaintance ever since.'

'Then why doesn't he speak?' asked the practical Lily.

'He's much too quick with his speech; and it's a very good thing he's a trifle quieter just now,' I said, sharply, and Lily looked at me and said, eagerly,

'Tell me all about it! Is he——'

'No, he is not.'

'Oh, I beg your pardon, Jane; I thought he was.'

An enigmatic dialogue, but we perfectly understood each other. And I hoped that I had made Lily understand I had no interest in Mr. Bird, for young girls jump so rapidly at conclusions where young men are concerned. Not that Lily was in the habit of jumping after young men in any way—I do not mean to convey *that* impression. Lily was full of spirits, but a good girl in every respect, with not an atom's worth of the ordinary Margate jetty girl in her constitution; not she. Still, curiously enough, I was deceived in and by Lily Brian. I had no idea she could have been so cunning or so easily deceived. One morning when I walked down the jetty, I found to my intense astonishment Mr. and Mrs. Brian, Lily, George, the eldest Master Brian, and Mr. Goode, all talking and laughing with Mr. Bird, and taking it in turns to peer through his telescope at some object on the far horizon. I walked up slowly, and with blushes on my cheeks, I am sure, in my surprise.

'Lily, my dear, here's a gunboat,' said Mr. Brian, as I approached; 'this gentleman has been kind enough to allow us to inspect it through his very powerful telescope. Look here, child.'

Mr. Bird did smile a little, in a sheep-faced and embarrassed kind of manner, as he glanced towards me, but he did not say a word when Mr. Brian handed me the instrument. He even let Mr. Goode focus the instrument for me without interfering in any way, although I fancied I heard him grinding his teeth.

'It's a capital glass, sir,' said Mr. Brian to him. Mr. Brian, being of a genial turn, was always disposed to be friendly with the first stranger whom he encountered out of town.

'Yes, it's a good glass.'

'Had it long, sir? Would you like to dispose of it now?' was the insinuating inquiry.

'It belonged to my father,' was the reply,

'therefore it has not a money value to me. It was his present when I was one-and-twenty, and I shouldn't like to part with it.'

Another birthday present, I thought. Heavens, if he was to lose this too !

'Certainly not, certainly not,' said Mr. Brian; 'I admire your good feeling, sir. George, you hear that,' he said to his son, who was wholly lacking in filial sentiment, and was at that identical moment sucking the bare knob of his stick as if it was an egg.

George nodded and then winked at me. A most objectionable lout was George, and Mr. Bird scowled ferociously at him, and from him to me.

I inspected the gunboat, or tried to inspect it, for the object-glass was very misty with little transparent worms that seemed to be wriggling and dancing all over it; I returned the telescope to its owner, who said, 'Thank you, ma'am,' very quietly, and with his look of sadness highly developed again.

Still he remained remarkably non-obtrusive; he did not attempt to force his conversation upon me in any way, and presently he was walking down the jetty with Mr. Brian, and talking and laughing as if he had known him all his life.

I thought all this was a new and deep-laid scheme of his, but it was really Lily Brian who was at the bottom of it all, or who at least induced her parents and her brother to say from that day 'Good-morning' to Mr. Bird, and even to shake hands with him. Hence I was obliged to say 'Good-morning' also when he directly addressed me, and to become by degrees on speaking terms with him again, and almost to forget that umbrella question which had been a bone of contention—a whalebone of contention—between us. Not that the umbrella was off his mind in any way, for he had been introduced to Captain Choppers on one occasion—by Captain Choppers's express request, as that gentleman wanted to borrow his telescope—and to my astonishment I heard Mr. Bird say, five minutes after the introduction,

'You see, it was not for the value of the umbrella, but because of the associations connected with it. I hope you understand, captain.'

'I understand perfectly,' was the reply; 'but that was no reason why you should have kicked up such an abominable uproar, sir.'

Captain Choppers had borrowed the telescope, and was now dominant and rude.

The time was drawing near towards the end of the holiday when Mr. Bird and I were friends. I may remark, actually friends, although I will say very firmly, and despite Lily Brian's opinion, nothing more than friends. Mr. Bird's holiday would expire a few days before our own, I learned, and, though I would not have owned it for untold wealth, I was sorry he was going back to London. He had informed me of his position by that time, and of his prospects for the future, or of some of them. He had given up the business, and his father's business before him, of carver and gilder in the Goswell Road; he was very clever at his trade, I felt sure, for he had been offered the post of superintendent of work by an eminent firm in Oxford Street, with whom he had done business for years, and at a very respectable salary indeed.

He was exceedingly communicative the last day of his stay in Margate; we were sitting together under the shelter of the verandah of the refreshment-room, with the band playing out in the rain. We were alone for a wonder; the Brians were on the rocks in search of anemones, with the exception of Lily, who had left me half-an-hour ago, with an injunction to come home if it 'poured,' and with an umbrella to shelter me, as I had ventured out without my own. She had seen—having very sharp eyes of her own—Mr. Geoffry Bird advancing down the jetty, and had made some trivial little excuse to leave me, 'to give the poor fellow a chance,' she told me afterwards. And there he was sitting by my side, cool and comfortable, and with the rain coming down in big drops and startling and confounding the pleasure-seekers.

'I shall be quite the gentleman soon, Miss Neild,' he said, with a laugh, 'and with a soul above shopkeeping. I only want a few friends about me to make life worth living, but I have never had any friends. Never had the time, or never saw anybody who was worth taking any trouble about, until—until lately.'

I could not reply to this. I did not know what he meant by 'lately.'

'People never took to me either,' he confessed, ruefully; 'I have a bad habit of speaking out what is on my mind, and I'm inquisitive and suspicious at times, and so forth. Altogether a beastly character.'

He waited for me to reply to this. I had thought him abrupt and inquisitive and suspicious, but that seemed a very long time ago now. He had improved *wonderfully* of late days; there were little traits of character, of frankness, earnestness, generosity, one could almost admire, but I was not going to tell him so, though he waited patiently as if he expected something of the kind. As if men were not vain enough in themselves, without being told of their accomplishments!

'You would not like anybody to say that but yourself,' I said, however; and it was a remark which did not commit me to anything.

'No. I should knock him down probably,'

he replied, 'especially if it were the captain or that railway goods inspector fellow.'

'Don't you like them?' I asked, innocently.

'Do you?' he rejoined.

'They are old friends, almost.'

'You don't make your lodgers your friends?' he remarked.

'Not always.'

'I should think not,' he said, very scornfully now.

'But these two gentlemen knew me when I was a little girl.'

'Ah! That makes a difference, I suppose; that's why they are both so fond of you,' he added, with a sigh.

'Fond of me!'

'You might marry either of them to-morrow, if you cared to hold up your little finger—I can see that.'

'What nonsense!'

'Oh! it's true enough,' he cried.

I laughed.

'Then I sha'n't hold up my little finger.'

'That's right,' he said; and he actually drew

a long, deep breath, as though it relieved him to hear me say so; 'for that captain's a pompous old noodle—a selfish party, who's stuck to my telescope a whole week—and the railway man would fidget any woman out of her life in a fortnight.'

'What's the matter with him?'

'He's an old woman, that's all.'

'Upon my honour, you are very uncomplimentary in your verdict upon my lodgers.'

'I hate your keeping a lodging-house,' he muttered.

'My poverty, and not my will, consents,' I answered.

He was very silent for a long time now. The visitors had hurried homewards, or had sought shelter like ourselves, the band had ceased playing, the rain was coming down in earnest.

'May I ask a favour of you before I go back to London?' he said, suddenly and very hoarsely.

'What is it?'

'Will you say "yes"?'

'Not till I know what it is about,' I replied, with spirit, 'certainly not.'

'Well, then,' he cried, 'don't give me back that little bird I carved. You said you would, and it has been preying on my mind that it will come flying back some day when I least expect it, and so upset me terribly. I want it hanging on your wall, to remind you of me sometimes, you know; being a *bird* like me, you see, it must. And though our acquaintance did not commence auspiciously, still you have forgotten and forgiven, haven't you?'

'Well—yes—almost.'

'And you'll keep that little carving?'

'Perhaps I will.'

'Bless you, Jane—Miss Neild, I mean. And now——'

I was getting alarmed at his vehemence, and very much afraid of what he would say next. I jumped up.

'I think I will go home to Lily. She's all alone, poor girl.'

'But it's raining cats and dogs.'

'I don't mind the rain, and I'm fond of cats and dogs,' I said, tripping from the shelter, and struggling to open the umbrella which Lily had lent to me.

'You have caught cold in the rain before now,' he said, drily, 'do stop a few minutes longer.'

'No,' I said, shaking my head, 'I would rather not.'

'Here, let me manage that thing for you, then,' he said, making a dash at the umbrella, opening it, and holding it above my head, 'if you must run away; but you'll get very wet.'

'I've got my waterproof.'

'Yes, but—oh, Lord!'

'What is the matter?' I exclaimed, as he turned very red and white, just as I had seen him on the Fort, only now he looked at me as if I were a ghost, and my spectral appearance had frightened him.

He did not reply at once, and I cried,

'Oh! what is the matter? Aren't you well? Won't you tell me?'

'It's all right—that is, I shall be all right in a minute,' he answered, in quite a new and hard tone of voice; 'don't mind me.'

'What can it be?'

'I tell you it's nothing, Miss Neild,' he said.

'Don't take any notice of me, please. I had rather you didn't.'

It was a strange request, but I did not. I maintained a rigid silence, being a little nettled presently at his own silent movements at my side, his steady stare ahead of him, the stern expression on his face. He marched along in so grave and dumb a fashion at last, that I could have slapped his face for him. What did he mean by such behaviour, I wondered? At the end of the jetty he brought my heart into my mouth, by suddenly roaring out,

'No, I'll never believe it! It's magic, it's a lying dream, it's anything but this! I can't believe it of you—I'd rather jump into the sea than think it for another moment.'

'Think what? Good gracious! why don't you tell me?'

'Think that you have deceived me all the time. You, too, of all the lot of them!'

'What have I done, Mr. Bird?'

'This—this umbrella,' he cried.

'Well?'

'It—it's the umbrella 1 dropped down your

area! My father's present; I can swear to it anywhere. They're my initials on that silver collar, "G. B." Oh! heaven and earth, to fancy for one instant that you—Miss Neild, I am going raving mad. Look at it, look at it!'

I stared from him to the umbrella, which he had thrust into my hands, and felt going mad myself. I looked so terribly mean and guilty, and yet I was so perfectly innocent, and I did not want him now to have one thought against me. I was confused, I did not know how to explain; I felt too indignant in the midst of my grief even to try to explain; for he should not have jumped to conclusions in this way, but have waited, and—and then I burst into tears.

'Oh, pray don't cry,' he called out, 'for mercy's sake, don't, Jane; I don't care about the umbrella now, I don't mind your taking—'

'It's—it's not mine!' I screamed out at last. 'It was lent me by Lily Brian, because she thought it—it—it would rain before I got home. There!'

'Thank God! What an awful thief she is for

one so young,' he cried. 'I am so tremendously glad though, so awfully glad——'

'Take your umbrella,' I cried, pitching it at him; 'and I'm glad it's found too, very.'

'I don't mean I'm glad I've found it, but that you——'

'How dare you suspect me?' I cried, sweeping majestically away from him, but he followed me, and held the umbrella over my head again, and overwhelmed me with hurried and incoherent apologies, which I declined to accept.

'Perhaps it's not mine,' he said at last. 'Pray be rational, Miss Neild, " B " stands for Brian as well as Bird. Is Mr. Brian's Christian name George, do you think?'

'Don't speak to me. You know it's your umbrella.'

'It *is* a little like it,' he said, dismally.

'I don't want any miserable evasions, Mr. Bird, and I never want to see or speak to you again, and I——'

'Why, Jenny, what's the matter?' cried Lily Brian, suddenly appearing round the corner of the street, and under another umbrella, and with a shawl over her arm. 'Where *have* you been ? Ma was afraid you wanted more wraps, and has sent me out with them, and—how d'ye do, Mr. Bird? Who'd have thought of seeing *you* this wet day ?'

'I've offended Miss Neild,' he said, not smiling in the least at her arch manner of address to him.

'You! Oh, what about ?' she cried.

'That nasty, hateful umbrella,' I said. 'Where did you get it, Lily? oh! where did you get it ?'

'What's the matter with the umbrella ?' asked Lily, very cool and self-possessed.

'It—it's not yours !' I exclaimed, 'it never was yours ?'

'No, it's George's. He lent it me this morning.'

'And where—where did your brother get it ?'

'I don't know.'

But we did very shortly. George had found it in his father's area, and, with a total disregard of other people's rights—being young, and short of umbrellas—had quietly appropriated it without any fuss. It was like a merciful dispensation having his initials already engraved for him, too.

Yes, it was down Mr. Brian's area that Mr. Bird had dropped his umbrella that night, and Geoffry had knocked at the next door by mistake.

I call him Geoffry now. And a very lucky mistake it was, he always says, even to this day, and I have been Mrs. Bird three years, and there is another little Bird crowing in its nest too.

A PRISON FLOWER.

A PRISON FLOWER.

CHAPTER I.

CHILD OR WOMAN.

THE sun was shining brightly in the airing-yard of one of our great Government prisons, and the 'children of the night,' poor, forlorn, purposeless women most of them, were plodding round their allotted space in the mill-horse fashion patent to the place, with the matron, a vigilant atom of humanity, in the background. It was early spring-time, and cold even in the sunshine, and the women, under their thick shawls, walked with briskness, as if anxious to get the hour's exercise over, as well as to put some extra degree of warmth into their bodies. It was the penal-class ward which was taking its exercise at this period when the curtain rises on our story, and the grim and lowering visages of the female prisoners stood almost as a warranty of the crime for which they were under lock and key for many years of their terribly wasted lives. They looked like beings without hope, or faith, or love; with hearts like the nether millstone, and on their rugged countenances was marked 'Dangerous' as clearly as though it were imprinted as a warning to all better folk brought into contact with them. Round and round, in Indian file, went the prisoners, stolid and silent, the rules against them as to conversation with each other. These were new-comers, of the worst class, or old offenders, or 'returns' from other prisons, where the lighter duties or the privileges of 'association,' had been abused, and so they were back again to the first and worst estate of penal servitude.

They were, taken altogether—taken mayhap without an exception—'a bad lot,' and the matron was wary of her black sheep. The prison was out of gear—'out of sorts'—that day, as it had been for weeks past, for the matter of that. Things had gone wrong generally; matrons and assistant-matrons had been changed; some new orders had been issued to the class which hated new orders; one or two of the women had broken out in defiance of them, and been carried to the 'dark cells,' and more than one life had been threatened for offences real or imaginary.

Even in the airing-yard there was an extra shadow cast, and the gloomy prison world was hardly working satisfactorily to prisoners or matrons, much less to the Honourable Board of Directors sitting in solemn conclave at Parliament Street, eternally studying the great question of 'Our Criminals'; the gigantic paradox of how these unruly souls shall live or die by rule.

Suddenly there appeared in the yard one prisoner a little behind time, and under escort of her officer—a new arrival, to whom rules were new and convict-life unknown; and it was her unlooked-for advent which turned the current of every woman's thoughts, and woke them up to life and wonderment and a strange excitement, for which even the matrons were wholly unprepared. For this was an innovation upon the monotony of prison service; a something new and unprepared for; a change in the affairs of those who were working out their sentences.

This was surely not a woman; rather a child; and even the matrons on duty, accustomed to cloak all feelings under official reserve, were taken off their guard. The new-comer was not fifteen years of age, but looked two good years younger. So child-like was her face and figure, and so short in stature was she, that the smallest sized prison dress in the establishment had had to be pinned up carefully round her to make even the semblance of a fit of it. A fair-haired, blue-eyed child was this too, whose proper place should have been at her mother's knees in some peaceful English home, rather than one more atom here of a world of crime and ignorance and horror.

The prisoners came, as if by one general instinct, to a full stop in the airing-yard; everything was forgotten but the presence in their midst of this new recruit to the ranks of the Devil's regiment, and the matron on duty, surprised even in her turn, omitted at once to remind them that they were infringing the great rule of the establishment. The child—for she looked no more than a child, and was at heart far less—had touched some unused chords in the wild nature of these prisoners; perhaps they had had sisters and daughters like her; they had been like her themselves before the world was steeped in murky darkness to them, and they knew what a terrible place it was, and how unfit for this young life. It was, even to the callous, sin-begrimed souls here, so awful a beginning to the little waif suddenly starting up amongst them, and proclaiming to them by her presence that she was one of them; just as bad as all the rest! One old woman who had lived in gaol almost all her life, and was prone to boast of her eight-and-twenty sentences, was the first to stop, horror-stricken, and arouse the attention of the rest.

'My God! look here,' she shrieked out across the airing-yard. 'Oh! just look here!'

'Silence!' exclaimed the matron, roused to a sense of the disorganisation gradually gaining the upper hand of all obedience to order. 'Silence, please.'

'Why, she's only a kid!' cried another. 'Oh, it's dreadful!'

'It's a shame—it was a burning shame to bring her here,' was the next exclamation.

'Wot's she done? Who is she? Here, let's have a squint at her, will yer,' cried a tall, raw-boned Lancashire woman, leaving the ranks and elbowing her way towards her.

'Why, it's like my own Bessie when I saw her last at home,' cried a fourth. 'I can't stand this; I can't look at her!'

'It's a shame,' welled forth the deep, hoarse murmur of the prison voices once again.

There were stifled sobs, suppressed cries of grief, even loud wailings and protestations against the enormity of the law which had placed this little stray in the great prison amongst them.

Meanwhile the subject of all this attention remained quiet and composed; she had even fallen into rank before the ranks had become broken up, and the matrons had grown nervous as to the ultimate result. It took but little to excite these women; they were always waiting, longing, and scheming for reaction.

'Take her back to her ward,' cried the matron in charge; and it was by only these means that some semblance of peace and concord was brought to the disorganised forces.

The child was hustled away, and, by dint of appeal and threat, the regiment of despair was once again formed into line, set slowly in motion, and proceeded on its monotonous tramp, tramp, tramp, round the big airing-yard.

The silent system was a delusion for the day; it was policy to ignore for a while the quick, short whispers of the prisoners when they thought themselves fairly beyond the earshot of their watchers. The element of discord had been removed, and in a few more minutes it was hoped that the women would settle down. Two prisoners, plodding on at the distance of a yard from each other, were the most talkative; one, the tall, Lancashire female already alluded to; the other, a thin, fragile being, of some two or three-and-twenty years of age, who had seemed to take less heed of the new-comer than the rest of her contemporaries. Only seemed—for there had been keen eyes which had taken stock of the latter prisoner, and ears which had heard one wild, heart-breaking cry escape her: a cry that had been wholly submerged in the Babel of sound which had broken loose. Finlanson, the Lancashire woman, remained still demonstrative; she who had the strength of a man, and was at times as violent as a man. Finlanson was sniffing very much, and occasionally wiping her eyes with the back of her hand in a quick, angry fashion.

'I'd like to smash the head in of that old judge who sent the kid on here,' she growled. ' I only wish he'd come in to see us, and I knew the bloke. He wouldn't get out alive, I'm reckonin'.'

' What business is it of yourn?' was the sharp answer back, and without looking round.

'It ain't nat'ral, Wilton, that's all; it ain't a bit nat'ral.'

'I daresay she's as bad as you are.'

'How do you make that out?'

'I don't know. Don't bother me about the gal,' said Wilton.

'Did you see what blue eyes she'd got? Blest if they wasn't like bits of chaney,' exclaimed Finlanson.

'I didn't notice.'

'I never felt so much like a babby in all my life as I do this blessed day,' Finlanson muttered. 'I——there's that cat of a matron looking at us.'

'I don't care for the matron,' Wilton responded, sullenly.

'No more do I. For two pins I'd fling that stone at her.'

'Oh, no, you won't; not while I'm here, you won't do that trick.'

'Won't I? You, you whipper-snapper, to talk to me. Take that!'

And, excited and out of temper, and readily impulsive, and altogether weary of the method

and monotony of an hour's exercise, Janet
Finlanson, taunted by Mary Wilton, brought
one large and heavy hand on the top of that
lady's big straw bonnet, and levelled her to
the ground.   Then began at once a second
scene of tumult with Janet Finlanson raving
like a mad woman, and threatening annihilation
to the authorities in general, with prisoners
siding for and against her, an alarm bell ringing,
and male warders from the men's side springing
up like magic and bearing off to solitary con-
finement the pugilistic and kicking Janet, 'put
out' by the mere entrance into prison service of
a girl of tender years, and not to be reduced to
a quiet state again for many desperate days of
insubordination and defiance.

Meanwhile Mary Wilton was picked up from
the ground and helped to her own cell, under
protest.   She was well enough—well enough to
'cut the heart out' of that Lancashire brute the
first time she came across her again.   'See if
she didn't!   See if she was going to be bashed
about for nothing by a common crittur like that!
Only just wait and see!'

It was on the cards that Mary Wilton, in her cell, and suffering from Janet Finlanson's unlooked-for assault, would prove herself another source of trouble presently to the authorities. She was excited and hysterical and hurt, and a little out of the common way had been known before to disturb the equanimity of Mary. But locked up in her cell, with her work ready to her hand, she, after a few minutes deliberation, thought better of it, and put down the metal 'pint' from which she had emptied some water on the floor, with the intention of battering at everything within reach. She sat down, snatched up her work suddenly, and after one little suppressed scream, with her face pressed against the mattress folded on the wall, so that no sound should well into the corridor, where the matron was on duty.

Had Miss Greenwood been listening without, she might have heard the following short soliloquy:

'No; I'll keep quiet for this once. To think that she's come, arter all. My little sister Daisy —just as she said she would!'

CHAPTER II.

ON NIGHT DUTY.

At nine o'clock in the evening there entered upon night duty a young and pretty—if a pale and delicate—woman, who at first sight seemed as singularly out of place in the precincts of a gaol, as little Daisy March had looked that morning. As she stood, talking to an officer before proceeding on her task of watch and ward, there 'seemed too much of the lady' in her to render the onerous duties of a prison fair and acceptable service; a common observer even might have perceived that this was some one from the better days, who, by a strange chance, or a strong motive—or, say even by a perverted taste—had been led to an uncongenial and unsatisfactory mode of life. The story may be faintly sketched forth presently, so far as it pertains to the chronicle which we have set ourselves to write, or affects the prison characters which will flit athwart our pages; therefore we need not enter into details here upon it.

Patience Greenwood had not been long in the service, and was, therefore, new to the rules. Night duty is the novitiate of the new officer—there is less upon the mind, less calls upon one's judgment in the dark hours with the wild beasts in their dens, asleep or feigning sleep, and, as a rule, particularly still. To a nervous matron, the night duty is probably a greater trial than the day's, but then one is not called upon to consider nerves in prison service. People with nerves are better out of it, and the less imaginative they are, probably the better too; and if it were possible in a young and thoughtful woman to submerge all sympathy with her surroundings, as one might sink a big stone to the bottom of the sea, why, in time she might become a model officer. But given nerves, and imagination, and a true woman's heart which will *not* grow callous with the callous and unyielding souls within her ken, and there is soon an end of it. The wheels grind heavily and harshly against each other, and their revolutions are fast and furious, till the final crash comes of the whole machinery.

Miss Greenwood was not a nervous matron for all this—on the contrary, one more self-possessed and calm it would have been difficult to match in the great gaol, but she possessed imagination, and mixed with a strong, religious feeling was that deep sympathy with the unfortunate which was at least against her becoming an every-day, mechanical officer. Still, these were early times, and she had not settled down yet; the prison world was strange and new to her, and even interesting. She was already considered very diligent and earnest—a new broom which had begun by sweeping cleanly. Presently, the old stagers thought, she would be like the rest of them—more matter-of-fact and less 'fine'—more like her sharp sister possibly, who had been a prison matron some two years and a half, and had all the rules and regulations

at her finger-ends. It was the elder sister whom
we have seen that morning in the airing-yard,
when the coming of Daisy March had seriously
upset the little amount of self-command of which
the female prisoners had to boast.

The younger Miss Greenwood proceeded
upon her night duty calmly and methodically,
making the *détour* of the prison, passing noise-
lessly and quickly from cell to cell, along corridor after corridor, listening once or twice to a
more than usually heavy sigh, or muttered
sleep-word, once exchanging a 'good-night'
with a restless soul, wide awake and staring,
and waiting for those two words from her, as
though in some way they were grains of comfort which a woman might take to heart and
sleep presently the better for. Down the dimly-
lighted wards to the corridor beyond and apart,
at the end of which were the dark cells, in the
days of which we write, proceeded the young
night officer. She closed the door after her as
she entered the passage, for Janet Finlanson
was bawling a ribald ditty at the top of her
voice, and accompanying herself with emphatic

kicks upon the wooden bench whereon she was lying full length. The dark cell had not daunted her; time had not weakened her voice, but only rendered her particularly husky, and her sense of injury was very strong upon her still. Janet Finlanson was making a night of it.

'Here—Hi! you Greenwood gal!' she shouted, directly the assistant-matron was in the ward, 'I know you're here. You can't *do* me; I want to speak to you.'

Miss Greenwood approached to listen to her complaint, and Janet Finlanson left off thumping with her heels in order to address her officer for awhile, and if the said officer were disposed to listen to her, which she was.

'I say, I've got a word or two for your sister.'

'Indeed.'

'She's dropped me into this mess, mind you. and I shall smash her when I get out,' said Finlanson; 'I'll smash her into atoms.'

'That is a poor message to give me, Finlanson,' said Patience Greenwood, quietly.

'Well, I mean it, and she'd better look out.'

'She will look out, although you don't mean it.'

'Don't I?' And here Finlanson was about to asseverate most solemnly and fiercely her fixed intention to 'do' for Miss Greenwood within the next seven days, when the young matron said 'Good-night,' in a quiet way that checked her. 'You ain't a-going?' cried Finlanson at once.

'Yes; I must not stop, you know.'

'Sometimes you stops longer,' remarked the prisoner. 'The last time I had a kick-up, and settled all the glass, you said as you was sorry.'

'I'm always sorry when you break out.'

'Good lor'—why?'

'Because you are so steady and straight-forward when you are going on well.'

Miss Greenwood knew the power of flattery over the majority of her sex, although there was truth as well as praise in her last assertion. No prisoner could behave better than Janet Finlanson when she liked—the pity of it was that she very seldom liked. Even when disposed to be diligent and placid she was to be turned into a fury by the least fancied slight from officer or fellow-prisoner, and without so much as a moment's warning of the transformation.

'Ah! yes; but the likes of you won't let us go on well.'

'Some of us try.'

'You do, p'r'aps.   I don't know no one else, and I likes you sometimes,' was the gruff response, 'but as for your sister——'

'Ah! you don't know what a good sister she is.'

'What did she want calling in the men, jest because I flattened Poll Wilton's bonnet? Mind yer, I shall kill Wilton, bang off.'

'Oh, no; you like her.'

'I shall suttingly kill Wilton,' persisted Janet. 'The likes of her a-talkin' about what she'll do to me, if I—but never mind that.   The imperence of her—why, I could blow her away at any moment.'

'Yes.   She is very weak,' said the assistant-matron.   'You must not be too hard upon her, Finlanson.   She thinks a great deal of you.'

'What next will you say?'

'She said she was very sorry you'd got into

the "dark," and it was all her fault.   She nearly
broke out, too, to join you.'

'Did she though?' said Finlanson, with a
great gasp, 'what, Poll Wilton?'

'Yes.'

'I don't see how you know, as you ain't in
her ward, and ain't on duty all day,' said Finlanson, suspiciously.

'My sister told me.'

'Ah! well, tell Wilton I don't mind a bit
then. I don't care what they do to me. I'm
strong as a 'ouse, and can keep it up. Here
goes agin.'

And Finlanson began to sing and scream and
hammer with her heels until Patience Greenwood said 'Good-night' once more.

'Oh! you're off then.'

'Yes, my head aches.'

'I won't make any row till you've got out of
the ward, jest because you haven't cut away
without saying a word to-night. But I shall
kill your sister, fust chance; see if I don't.'

These were Janet Finlanson's last words, but
they did not impress Patience Greenwood as

words uttered by women less demonstrative and more dangerous might have done. Finlanson was a big woman, with big words to match, but with an infinitesimal amount of brain, and some semblance of a heart left. An impulsive, spasmodic, awkward customer, this 'Lancashire lass' of fourteen stone, to whom the coming of a child to prison had been an offence and grievance only to be protested against by a meaningless outbreak on her own part. 'One of the worst of women,' was written against her in the prison-books, but this was hardly fair. 'One of the most unmanageable,' would have been a fairer criticism; but then there had been no one to manage and control this nature in its early stages—no one to love and rear her, and only the eternal horror of a bad example for ever set before her—examples of theft and profligacy, and even murder, in the dens of Liverpool, where she had been born and bred, and hence the result scarcely to be wondered at. Here was the natural outcome of neglect in one misguided nature. What the sum total is of such neglect amongst the poor and vicious, one reads whilst running past in fear of them. The prisons were always full in those days. The light of better times and truer thoughts shines even now but dimly over the waste land on which the darkness rests.

CHAPTER III.

THE PRISON DAISY.

WE, as faithful chroniclers, are somewhat disposed to assert that Patience Greenwood had at least not that supreme reverence for prison rules and regulations which a properly organised matron was expected to possess. Had she remained all her life—or the best years of her life—'under government,' it is doubtful if the reverence would have deepened very much. She was an eccentric young woman, and would have given trouble to the authorities by 'wanting to know, you know,'—by objecting to the rules, and possibly by sending in proposed amendments to them, by an absence of profound respect, mayhap, for principals, and an inner consciousness that they were but fussy, pompous, and common-place folk, take them altogether, to whom in her old and higher estate—from which a father's speculations had hurled down a family—she might have thought it preferable to hold aloof, or to laugh at good-naturedly, for their little vain displays of brief authority.

But she was fond of 'the service,' and with an honourable desire to be of service too, which is not always the incentive to exertion in the heart of every matron. She had a fair idea of what was duty, and she followed it to the best of her ability,—although it was remarked that she showed too much interest in the prisoners, talked too much to them at times, and had been even known to preach at them. Though a good officer, she was not likely to prove so sharp and efficient as her elder sister, it was thought. She would probably wear herself out quickly, taking things to heart too much as she did, and not getting used to the business so promptly as she might have done. Her sister Kate thought this, as well as many strangers with not half the interest in her, but Patience Greenwood only smiled, and continued the even tenor of her way.

Decidedly an inquisitive young woman, we may assert without exaggeration; and it was evident that Daisy March had aroused in her more than a common amount of interest. She would have been glad to know the whole story of this child of fourteen's appearance in gaol; and why the sentence had been so severe upon a girl so young. This was an impression which Patience could not shake from her mind—not even as it became fairly evident to the world about her that Daisy March was as wild and wilful, as resistive of all discipline, and as defiant of it, as women twice and thrice her age, and with twice and thrice her penal-servitude experience. Taken altogether, Daisy March was hardly an interesting character, people thought; she was only a specimen of one who had matured in crime with a more frightful rapidity than her fellows, and seemed at her early age as bad as any of them. The prisoners had soon grown accustomed to her, and their sympathy had evaporated as quickly as it had been shown on her first appearance in their midst; she was as sullen and harsh to them as to her officers, as ready to take offence, as watchful of every opportunity to deceive—the regular gaol-bird—and of the old, grim, regulation pattern.

Still, in the estimation of Patience Greenwood, there *was* something in her which was different from the rest—there was, even to the assistant-matron's mind, the certainty of a mystery about her presence there, which had not yet been fathomed.

'That girl March pretends to be worse than she is,' said Patience Greenwood one day to her sister.

'My dear Patience, how you worry about that prisoner. She cannot be a great deal worse, I fancy.'

'I am not so sure of it.'

'You must not be romantic in this sad business of our lives,' said the elder sister, 'or the work will become too much for you.'

'It is too much for me already.'

'You are not feeling ill?' asked Kate, anxiously.

'I don't know that I am feeling particularly strong,' was the reply.

'You will apply for sick leave, then. Go down to Aunt Mary's in the country. You must not give way.'

'Oh! I shall keep well,' said the younger sister: 'you and I cannot afford to fall sick. We must leave that luxury to the rich.'

'I don't quite understand you,' said Kate Greenwood, regarding her sister doubtfully; 'but I know that I am not going to have you killed by prison service. If you cannot get used to it—resign.'

'Have you got used to it?' answered Patience, with a visible little shudder.

'1 think I have.'

'Then I am sorry for you.'

'It is my " profession," ' said Kate, laughing, 'and I study it professionally.'

'If our poor, dear dad could only have known what was to become of us, Kate,' said Patience, half-slowly, half-drily, 'perhaps he would not have speculated in quite so many bubble companies.'

'Patience, I am sure you detest this life.'

'I don't like it a great deal,' was the confession; 'possibly for the reason I have already stated, that it is too much for me.'

'You will give it up?'

'Not yet.'

'Presently?'

'Yes—presently.'

·Before the long hours and the hard service render you unfit for anything else. Oh! Patience, you are all I have left in the world, and I cannot afford to lose you.'

Kate flung her arms round her, and kissed her. The elder sister was not an impulsive or demonstrative woman, but there was a true affection for the younger in her heart, one of those unfathomable loves which one sees at times—not too often—between sisters, and which, in its deep solemnity of devotion and self-sacrifice, amazes people of a colder stamp. And Kate Greenwood was devoted to this younger sister—had been as a mother to her in those tender years of girlhood, when the mother, by God's will, had been taken away from them both. Under the mask of her imperturbability, she was watching her sister every day with keen attention, and setting others on a friendly watch also.

Our dialogue had occurred in the little room of Patience Greenwood. It was Kate's 'night-off,' and she was spending an hour or two with her younger sister, whose time for going on night duty was approaching. The time passed quickly with them; they had had a great deal to talk about—of many little plans for the future, when, perhaps, they should be able to give up prison service altogether, and live somewhere in the country. This was Kate's day-dream, which rendered the present life endurable, and which kept Kate stronger than her sister Patience, whose day-dreams were hardly as bright, and who did not see the end of it so clearly as the other.

A few days afterwards, it was announced to Miss Patience Greenwood that she was to be transferred to another government prison in a pleasant London suburb, and Patience regarded the lady-superintendent a little doubtfully when the announcement was made to her.

'I would prefer to remain with my sister, Mrs. Edgar,' was Patience's slow reply.

'The order has come from Parliament Street, and there is no appeal,' said the lady.

Patience flew to her sister.

'You are at the bottom of this transfer, Kate, and it's no use denying it.'

'Well, I am,' the elder sister acknowledged. 'I was anxious about you, and spoke to the doctor. The new prison is on a more healthy site, and you will have a better chance of health.'

'This is our first separation, then ?'

'We are separated now, Patience,' was the other's reply, 'and we shall even meet more often under the new arrangement. Our "nights-off" will be the same, and we will spend them together.'

'I shall miss all the old faces,' said Patience. 'The matrons I have learned to like, and the prisoners who have become, as it were, my charge. I wonder what Daisy March will do without me.'

'Without you!'

'Well, she does mind what I say, now and then, I think.'

'My dear Patience, you have Daisy March upon the brain.'

And this Daisy March, whose name stands in this story as one of our principal characters—what of her? That young lady was in 'the dark' at the present moment, having tried the effect of a break-out, it was thought upon Janet Finlanson's earnest recommendation, who considered that it 'kept the pot a-bilin'.' But Daisy had especial reasons for this extraordinary ebullition of temper, and they were soon apparent to the night officer. Daisy March had been three months in prison at this time, we may add.

'I say, Miss Greenwood,' she said, in a low voice, when the 'inspection' had been opened, to see that the refractory prisoner was 'all right' in the dark cell to which she had been consigned, 'I want to speak to you.'

'Well?'

'I ain't to see much more on you, they say.'

'How do you know that?'

'You're goin' to t'other prison, ain't you?'

'Who told you?'

'Oh! it's all over the place, you can't keep things quiet here. I knowed it yesterday, and that's why I've got to "the dark."'

'You! And for what reason?'

'I could speak to yer, you see—I could——'

She paused, then went on again.

'I could tell you I was sorry you was a-goin', miss.'

'Why, you don't care for me?'

'Don't s'pose I care for nobody. Nobody at all; but I don't want you to go, somehow.'

'Why not?'

'You ain't like the rest on 'em,' she replied. 'You ain't like your sister—not a bit of it. Nobody likes your sister.'

'That's bad news to me.'

'You do, I s'pose?'

'Yes. She has been a good, kind sister to me.'

'Has she, really?'

'And you have a sister, who has been kind to you.'

'How—how do you know that?' cried Daisy, very quickly now. It was her turn to be surprised at the information.

'I have fancied it,' said Patience Greenwood, drily.

'You knows too much for me,' said Daisy March; 'you are precious artful, if——'

'If I sometimes think I can guess the reason why you are here.'

'Well, what was it?'

'Because your sister was here too. And you were rash enough, and wicked enough, to join her at any cost.'

'You know a lot, you do,' said Daisy, ironically.

'Am I wrong?'

'Well, Poll wos allers good to me. She took my part—fought with father for me, scratched mother, did everythink for me—and as I couldn't get on without her, why, I came here. That's it. And you won't split, will you?'

'And you are fond of this sister, then?'

' I jest am !'

' Why do you break out like this, then ? Mary Wilton doesn't.'

' Oh, she puts me out, though ; she talks to the other women too much,' Daisy added, jealously, 'and I can't bear it. But,' she added, quaintly, ' I came here to see you this time, and I'm werry comforbul. *I like this shop !*'

' Horrible !'

' And I shall come and see you in your new crib,' said Daisy, positively. ' I goes in for a bran new leaf to-morrow. I shan't be werry long afore I follow you, you see.'

' Ah ! you'll have to be very good, March, to get to the next prison.'

' You'll see.'

' You can be good if you like, then ?'

' You jest see !' was the strong reiteration here. ' Poll's going, and now you're going, and —I mean it now.'

' Mean it always, Daisy March, and I shall be very glad,' said our heroine, earnestly.

' You glad ! What if I—— Here, did you say glad ?'

'Yes, very glad.'

'Well, you are a rum un,' was the inelegant response, in a low, sepulchral, wondering tone of voice. 'I don't make it out, you know.'

'Why I should be glad?'

'Zackly so, miss. Because you see I'm so awful bad; born bad, without a scrap of good in me anywhere. They'll tell you so in Scroggs's Court, Liverpool, and no flies. They'll tell you there——'

'I don't want to hear what they say of you there, Daisy. Never mind them. What they say of you here is another matter, and I shall be glad when you have your good conduct badge. I'm going now. Good-bye.'

'Good-bye for the present, miss. That's all?'

'That's all.'

'And you will be glad to see me?'

'Yes, very glad.'

'Thankee, thankee. God bless you, miss. I don't make it all out, but God bless you. There!' shrieked the girl.

The matron walked away slowly, stopped, came back again.

'What made you say that?' she asked.

'I don't know. I've heard people talk like that, off and on.'

'Do you know what it means?'

'Dashed if I do.'

'Do you know anything of Him whom you call upon to bless me?'

'No.'

'Not anything?—oh, not anything?'

'The parson's been a tryin' to make me know a bit, and I've been a tryin' to understand him —but lor, bless you, there's no making him out, miss; try as hard as you can.'

'You will understand, I hope. Meanwhile, God bless Daisy March for trying. I think He will in His good time.'

And Patience Greenwood moved slowly away —moved on for ever from this neglected prison flower. Matron and convict had made many plans, and looked forward to the future. But the future is God's, and belongs not to man or woman.

CHAPTER IV.

DAISY IS DECEIVED.

STEP by step, to trace the prison life of Daisy March, and to track her faltering, feeble progress—but still a progress—in detail, comes not within the province of a story of this kind. It will be sufficient to record that a wild, distorted nature put forth some green young shoots towards the light and life lying beyond the murky world in which she had been cast, and that she showed some little efforts to work upwards. And if this was not repentance, and there was no religion in the question, if the chaplain of the gaol exercised no power over her, and was at any opportunity an object to be ridiculed and scoffed at, still Daisy March worked on doggedly, learned some lesson of self-restraint, gathered to herself the fact that, by good behaviour and fair obedience, the distance between the penal class and ' the association '—the prison, wherein the rule was silence and severity, and the prison beyond, where silence would be the exception —grew less and less with every day. The good conduct badge was earned at last, and it was on the cards that Daisy March might be transferred at any moment. There had been every incentive to exertion ; her sister had gone, and was a 'Number One woman' in the new prison, and Patience Greenwood was waiting for her, she was sure. It had been a promise between them, and the young assistant-matron had been the only officer to give her a good word. This sister of hers—this Kate Greenwood—was not one of the right sort. She was ' down on her '; she was all for the rules; she was more like a machine than an officer ; she seldom smiled, and was always very silent, watchful, cross; she gave her no news of the ' other one '; not she, without it was wrenched out of her.

Once or twice in odd opportunities to say a

few words, when Daisy March had become a prisoner over whom a less amount of rigour was exercised, when she was a 'cleaning woman,' and allowed a few half-hours of liberty about the wards, efforts were made by her to render Kate Greenwood conversational.

'You don't tell me anythink about her, Miss Greenwood,' she said once; 'I don't know nothin'.'

Miss Greenwood regarded her very thoughtfully, and, as Daisy March considered, very crossly, being a bad judge of the looks of earnest folk.

'What do you want to know, March?'

'She's at the other prison, I s'pose?'

'My sister?'

'Yes.'

'She is in the country now,' was the reply; 'at her aunt's.'

'There, now; blest if I didn't think there was some game up. What's the use in her bein' away when I'm a-goin' to her directly? What's the——'

'She has been ill,' said Kate Greenwood, interrupting her.

'You don't say that!'

'But she is getting better, they say. She will be on duty next week again, I hope.'

'Why didn't I know this afore? Why couldn't you tell me?' said Daisy March, almost peremptorily.

'I am not here to give you news,' was the cold answer; 'and, besides,' she added, 'it might have unsettled you.'

'Oh! much you cared about that.'

'And,' she continued, very calmly, and quite oblivious to the taunt conveyed, 'I wanted you to get to *your* sister.'

'Oh! she's told you that, then, has she?' exclaimed Daisy.

'No; I told her long ago,' was the reply.

'Ah! you're too sharp for me, Miss Greenwood,' remarked the other. 'And what's she doing?'

'She is doing pretty well.'

'It's funny you're having a sister and me having one, too, and all going on together like a four-in-hand; ain't it?'

'I don't see the fun in it.'

'It's funny to me, and no mistake. You don't know——'

'I know you are talking too much,' said the matron, closing the subject suddenly and peremptorily. 'There, get on with your work.'

'Ah! I shall never like you a bit,' muttered Daisy March to herself; 'and, what's more, I shan't try.'

The impression even grew upon Daisy March that she disliked this officer more with every day, and that the prim young matron evaded her, and took a deal of pains to keep out of her way, a tremendous deal of pains, as though she hated to say a word to her, or give her one scrap of news. Thank goodness, she should soon be out of her clutches, soon have earned her right to get away to the prison where the other was, and where the rules were not so hard and fast, or 'down upon a gal.' She should like that new prison, she was sure; she would be presently in association there, and allowed to talk a bit, and she was 'uncommon fond' of talking, if they would only let her.

'There was a great deal to perplex this half-child, half-woman. She did not quite make everything out. Miss Greenwood was not seen for days together; then she took her fortnight's holidays, and came back, looking all the worse for them. There was something wrong somewhere, she thought; and one early morning Daisy seized her opportunity and made a dash at her in the ward:

'How is she? You don't tell me nothin', you don't,' was the old charge against the matron.

Miss Greenwood turned white, but she was very calm, and even firm.

'How is your sister, do you mean?' she said, interrogatively.

'No, no, yours; is she well?'

'She is very well,' came the slow answer, which was accompanied by a swift walk away from her questioner, with whom she would hold no further converse, it was evident, that day.

'Stuck up; allers so drefful stuck up. I do hate the sight o' you, and no mistake,' Daisy March said, shaking her fist after the matron.

A few days afterwards there came back to the

old prison big Janet Finlanson, the woman who had broken out into a fit of passion because so young a prisoner as Daisy March had fallen into the custody of the State. Janet had worked her way almost by a miracle to the secondary stage of prison servitude, but it had been more than a miracle to keep her subservient to the rules there. She had had her feelings hurt; there had been a great deal to upset her in Poll March's behaviour, and she had shivered all the glass in the kitchen with her broom one day instead of doing her work, and had tried to knock Poll March's brains out against the wall for sending her contemptuous messages, and returning the lock of her hair which she had given her, covered thickly with salt.* Janet had been sent back to the penal ward, with her badge stripped from her, and all her hard work to begin over again. She did not care, she said; nobody should trample upon her; and as she had come back, by jingo, they should have a

---

* An insult which one female convict will occasionally offer to another, and which invariably leads to much heart-burning and passionate outbreaks.

time of it—the lot of 'em! And a time of it
they had.

Still, Daisy March found an opportunity to
communicate with Janet Finlanson. In a 'stiff'
—which is the cant name for a written missive
surreptitiously conveyed from one prisoner to
another, and faithfully passed on till it reaches
the hands of her for whom it is intended—
Daisy, who could write a little now, asked two
questions—

'Was Poll hurt? How was the Greenwood
girl?'

She did not get her answer readily. It was
three days coming back, and was at last taken
from under the back hair of a prisoner, and
surreptitiously conveyed to her.

Here is the letter, the ink manufactured from
the smoke gathered at the bottom of a 'pint'
which had been held over the gas-jet in the
cell, and the paper a torn fly-leaf of her Bible.
Janet Finlanson had been taught to write and
spell in prison, and here is a fair specimen of
her powers of composition :

'*Pol's bad. Lade up. She sint mi air bac*

*sallted, an' I rushed 'er fur it. She won't cheek
mee agane. 'Ope I ain't urt her to mutch. i doant
no wot u mene by ows the other grenewood. She's
ded.'*

Daisy March deciphered this epistle with
great difficulty, but, when it was mastered, she
was more like the child she looked than she
had ever been yet—a child in her passionate
abandonment to grief and the extravagant
misery of her despair. There were strange
depths of feeling, wild and incomprehensible
and unfathomable in this untaught nature, but
they displayed themselves only in the old, sad,
mad fashion of our female prisoners. Daisy
March 'broke out;' the glass within reach was
shattered, the metal pint was battered out of
shape, the blankets were torn into a hundred
strips, and fighting, kicking, and screaming, this
distraught child was carried to the penal cell
out of the way of women striving to do well,
but terribly quick to follow an evil example,
and only too ready to fling away all sense of
self-restraint.

It was a source of regret to more than one

female officer that Daisy March had broken out again. The extreme youth of the prisoner had always stood in her favour, and enlisted the secret sympathy of the matrons in her anomalous position; there had been no little satisfaction at the child prisoner becoming more childlike and natural with the teaching of the gaol. And now it had all to be begun again—and the weary, heart-sickening, hope-deferred task, to start afresh from the very beginning of this miserable, soul-shadowing existence.

'They told me a lot o' lies; they kep it all from me, an' she was dead all the while. I won't go to any other prison now. I'll die here, if I can. I won't care for anythink or anybody ever any more. I won't—I won't—I won't!'

The matron on duty came to see her every hour, and strove to pacify her, but she would not listen to a word. She was a fury, who might scream herself to death in time—a demoniac, and not human in her ravings. The disappointment was hard to endure. Heaven knows what thoughts had been in this young girl's mind concerning her new life in prison, her better life beyond it, and she did not bear this disappointment well. She gave way completely—so very completely that even the matrons, accustomed to these scenes, became alarmed, and the prison surgeon regarded her as a being whom it was difficult to comprehend, and beyond his power, as it seemed, presently to save.

No one had imagined that Daisy March would have taken the matter to heart; she was a prison item, nothing more, and not to be credited with more human feeling than the rest of them, and indeed, in the early stages of her career, she had shown herself in many things particularly callous. But Daisy March was not to be measured by the square and rule, and no one understood her yet. The suspicion that this was a character out of the common order had been guessed at faintly, perhaps, by Patience Greenwood, sleeping now peacefully in a country churchyard, with all the dangers and difficulties of prison service for ever far removed from her.

Daisy March refused all food—fought with

those who endeavoured to give it her—was found at last lying like a dead thing in her cell, and was carried to the infirmary, where she battled with a raging fever, and the bodily weakness following the fever, for many a long day.

CHAPTER V.

THE INFIRMARY CELL.

CLOSELY attached to the infirmary of the prison were several cells, whither were drifted those invalids whose refractory nature would resist even the mild rules of the doctor, and 'break out' on the sick beds, to the distress and discomfort of their fellow prisoners about them. Such women would be removed to large and airy cells away from the general ward, and here the ordinary attendant, very often a prison cleaner, who had been promoted for 'sobriety of conduct,' or general good behaviour, would wait upon them, or occasionally a special attendant in those extraordinary cases which are patent to gaol life as elsewhere.

Cases of infection would be isolated thus, of course, and Daisy March's had become one of these. Hers had been a terrible fever, and the authorities had become greatly alarmed for the safety of their large flock of black sheep, and hence Daisy March, on coming to herself, found that she was the inmate of a large, well-ventilated room, or cell, wherein was plenty of space, and light, and air; and that this cell was her own exclusive, private apartment, for her sole use and benefit, and with the luxury of a special attendant to her needs.

And that special attendant, sitting with her back towards her, seemed, to the half-dazed intellect of Daisy March, something like a figure she had seen before, although, mayhap, a dream figure, one of the many by which she had been lately most terribly perplexed, and which took all shapes and every conceivable and inconceivable form and face, from Patience Greenwood's, the woman who was dead, to those 'pals' of the Liverpool dens, from which, for a time, the hand of the law had snatched her away.

She was too weak to speak, so she lay and

wondered till her weakness led her to close her eyes, and finally to faint. And so on for a day or two, with the attendant very calm and self-possessed and watchful, until some slight renewal of vitality gave the sick girl strength to speak.

Then came the words out, very low and falteringly, and with a ring of wonderment in them which was not to be repressed.

'You are her sister, then?'

'Yes, her sister.'

'And where's this? Prison still?'

'This is one of the infirmary cells,' was the reply.

'And you—what's put you here?'

'I will tell you when you are stronger. Not now.'

'I don't want to be no stronger. I don't want to hear anythink about you. I won't— I——'

'Hush, hush!' said Kate Greenwood, rising and bending over her. 'You forget I have a deal to tell you, when you are a little better.'

'A deal to tell me?' repeated Daisy March, slowly.

'Yes.'

'About *her*, do you mean?'

'Yes, about her. She charged me to deliver you a message.'

'Honour bright?'

'Yes—honour bright,' replied Kate Greenwood, earnestly.

'Becos you're such a liar, you are,' murmured Daisy March.

The matron winced at this plain-speaking.

'Why do you think that?' she asked, softly.

'You told me she was well—very well, you said; and all the time she was dead and gone. And you knew she was!' cried Daisy March, fretfully.

'There, there, you must not grow excited, Daisy,' said Kate, in a low tone. 'I was asked not to tell you—it was her wish that you should not know till you had gone to the.new prison. And she *was* well, I think, in Heaven.'

'You were not to tell me?'

'No; I was not to tell you.'

'That's queer. Let me know all about it to-morrow, please, when I'm a bit less like a babby. Will you?'

'Yes.'

But on the morrow she was ill again, and it was feared that the relapse would carry Daisy March away before the message from the dead could be delivered to her. The morrow brought a faint ray of hope again, and though she did not get rapidly strong, though it seemed as if it were destined that health and strength should come no more to her, still she lay a fragile and faint semblance of life at last, and with the courage to hear the story out. And this was it, told by white, quivering lips, and from an earnest woman's heart.

CHAPTER VI.

THE MESSAGE FROM THE DEAD.

'You wasn't to tell me, you say. And why?' was Daisy March's inquiry, when she was well enough to hear the story.

'Lest it should lead you to break out, just as it did after all when it was told you by Finlanson. My poor sister Patience was very anxious you should get away from here,' replied Kate Greenwood; 'here were the worst of prisoners, and you were very young.'

'Was she anxshus?' murmured the sick girl. 'Well, I thought she took to me a bit; I did, indeed. She was not like any of the rest of you; no, that she wasn't.'

'And on being transferred to the other prison,

Daisy, my sister had hoped that you would remain; passing on in time to Fulham Refuge, and from the Refuge to an honest life beyond it,' continued the matron.

'The likes o' that now. To think all that of me, as if it could be done!'

'And I should have told you of this before you went away, giving you her message, when you were stronger of heart and had more self-control,' said Kate. 'Do you understand me?'

'I think I do. Go on, please, and don't give me too many hard words, if you can help it.'

'When my sister Patience lay dying, she thought of you very deeply. You seemed to be as a part of her life, which I had never known. She had had strange hopes about you —a strong wish to rescue you from the old life that has sent you here, poor child. Had she lived, she would not have lost sight of you; and when your four years had been served, Daisy, she, with God's great help, would have striven very hard to make you better than you are; to put you in a fair way of beginning life again, and beginning it well.'

'She was very good,' said the sick girl, thoughtfully; 'but——'

'But?' repeated Kate Greenwood.

'But it couldn't have been done, at no price!'

'Yes—yes—it could have been done,' said Kate Greenwood, quickly.

The girl lay and regarded the excitement of her nurse with a faint and wondering interest; but she said again:

'I shouldn't have been up to growin' good, like those poor critters in the tracts the lady comes and reads to us,' said Daisy March; 'I wasn't born good no how. We've never had a good 'un in our family: nothing like one.'

'Then you must leave the family, Daisy; get away from all of them.'

'It ain't easy that,' was the reply; 'they likes me, and I likes them. They'd do anythink for me, the lot on 'em, though we fight orful at times.'

'And " the lot "—who are they?'

Daisy thought the matron particularly curious, but she answered, very readily:

'There's the guv'nor, but he's at Portland

jest now; and mother—she keeps 'ouse, and looks arter me, and Poll, and Tom, and Teddy, when she can.'

'When she is out of prison herself?' added Miss Greenwood.

'Ex'axly.'

'And when in prison?'

'Ah! there it is.　Then we gets into a mess, and that's 'ow Poll got here.　And as I missed Poll dreadful—for she's been allers kind to me, she has—I thought I'd come in arter her.　And much good that's done,' she added, querulously —'and much I've seen on her!'

'Perhaps that's for the best.'

'Oh! it's easy to say that; but didn't you like *your* sister?' said Daisy March, with the blue eyes keenly watching over the coverlet.

'Yes,' was the reply, 'she was a good woman.'

'I knows it,' answered Daisy; 'and Poll's a bad 'un.　And bad 'uns like each other, too; they can't help it, I s'pose, sometimes.　And,' continued Daisy, warming with her subject, 'Poll allers took my part becos I was a little 'un, and fought 'em all round at times, guv'nor and all; and when she was tooked, and I was left with Tom and Ted, I thought I'd rather come here jest for peace and quietness; and here I am.'

'Out of love for your sister?' inquired Kate Greenwood.

'I don't quite know what it wos for now; I tried to be caught, and it didn't take a long while to catch me, did it?' she added, with a feeble little laugh; 'it was the sixth case agin me, and I caught it hot; jest as I calkylated.'

Kate Greenwood regarded her attentively; even critically. In the matron's mind were many thoughts and doubts, and the child's character was difficult to comprehend. There were lights and shades in it, though the shades were terribly predominant, and only a faint thread of gold, here and there amidst the darkness, told of the good that might have been, with other hands leading her away from—instead of towards—the terrible pitfalls about her desolate young life. To look now so very fair, and gentle, and bright, and to have known only the ghastly experience of sin, and to have been trained to theft as to something that paid, even taking into account the 'bad luck' against it sometimes, and the accumulation of the sentences against it, leading at last to penal servitude. Not fifteen years of age yet! and presently to go into the world with no better thoughts or fairer hopes than when she had been locked up away from it. The matron had had experience herself of prison characters, had witnessed much defiance of good, the cunning to resist right, the awful callousness to all impressions which sought to convey one idea of God, or hope of heaven; and of the power of these lower and benighted natures to reform at all, she had become a little sceptical. She had seen a great deal of hypocrisy, and no true penitence, and hence had grown—albeit a good and earnest woman—somewhat callous in herself, the natural outcome possibly of the life which she had chosen, or necessity had chosen for her.

But there had come a change to her, too, though she hardly knew the length and breadth of it yet; in her sister's thoughts, her sister's death, she had witnessed a more earnest and hopeful nature than her own, and it had softened and impressed her; teaching her the lesson of true sympathy for the poor humanity about her, and pointing out the way, at times, to be of service to it.

It was as if some of the kindly Christian virtues of the younger woman had fallen to Kate Greenwood as a legacy, which she would treasure all the more out of the deep love for her to whom it had belonged.

'I wish you wouldn't stare at me like that,' said Daisy March at last.

'Was I staring?' murmured Kate; 'I did not know it.'

'You wosn't thinkin' of me, I fancy. Poll stares like that at times. Poll agin!' said Daisy, fretfully. 'Blest if I can keep her out of my 'ed at all to-day.'

'I was thinking of my sister, too,' said Kate at last, 'and in what way I should deliver you her message.'

'You've been a long while giving it a body.'

'I have.'

'Go on, please. I 'spose there's a sermon in

it; but I can bear her preaching now. I liked her,' said the child prisoner, very thoughtfully again.

'No, Daisy March, the sermon was for me, and I have profited by it. It was to me she preached, and taught me courage, and faith, and perseverance. Her message to you was this; "Trust in my sister Kate; she takes my place, and will save you if you will try to save yourself."'

'Is that all?' said Daisy March, somewhat disappointed, 'becos I don't know as how I make it out.'

'And she bade me say with all her heart, what you said once to her, "God bless you."'

The girl was very silent for a while now, and closed the blue eyes, over which the long lashes quivered painfully. When she opened them again, she said:

'I am to trust you then? She said so?'

'If you will.'

'What are you goin' to do with me?'

'Pray for you. Teach you to pray for yourself.'

'I'm too old for that *fun*; I know I am.'

'You are not yet fifteen?'

'Yes; but then I never wos a child, you see,' she answered, moodily ; 'and what are you goin' to make out of me here——'

'Oh! not here, so much,' cried Kate, seizing her opportunity, 'but away from here, if you will come to me when the old, bad life lies further back, and the light shines upon the new : the light of Heaven, Daisy. For'—she added, after a pause—'I am going away.'

'Going away; you, too !'

'I shall be waiting for you, as I promised my sister Patience that I would, under any circumstances,' she said; 'and you will come to me a better woman.'

'I can only try,' murmured Daisy March.

'And you *will* try ?'

'Yes.'

'That is a promise. We can talk more of this before I leave for good. I am hardly of the service now, and only here by a kind permission to act as nurse to you until you are strong again.'

VOL. I.   S

'Oh! I don't want to get strong if you're a-goin' when I'm well.'

'For the sake of her we have lost, get strong in health, and so strong in the good purpose to begin life afresh.'

'I can but try,' said the child prisoner again, and in a lower voice.

'And try you will,' was whispered back again, and as the old response to her.

'Yes,' answered Daisy, for the second time, 'jest as if she was a-watchin' on me, as they say God watches; don't they?'

'Yes, always.'

'All right. I make it out a little now, I think.'

CHAPTER VII.

MISTRESS AND MAID.

IT is not necessary to dwell at much greater length on the prison life of Daisy March, though this is a story of the prison-land. It will suffice for the clearer explanation of our narrative to say that Daisy March came by slow degrees to convalescence, even to a fixed resolution to amend, backed by the hope of future peace, the fair promise of a home, the fairer promise of a friend. She became one of the few female convicts—terribly few, alas!—who, without hypocrisy, *do* make an earnest, upward effort, and awaken to the sense of the horrors by which they have been surrounded and the evils from which it is in their power to escape. She awoke

to penitence ; she learned diligently to read and
write now.; she became one of the most promis-
ing of the prison school ; she read, and presently
she understood her Bible ; the misty land of doubt
and despair receded further and further back,
and the life in store for her grew brighter as she
gazed towards it.

She grew up a fair young woman with a very
sad and thoughtful face—they called her the
Prison Daisy, or the Prison Flower—and her
fellow convicts were proud of her, despite all her
efforts to keep good, and show herself 'Oh ! so
much better,' they added, scoffingly, 'than anybody else.' It was these scoffs which were
hardest to bear up against, as they came also
from her sister, of whom she was very fond, for
whose sake she had sinned to share her prison-
home, and who, having never recovered from
her last conflict with Janet Finlanson, was almost
a confirmed invalid. Presently 'Mary Wilton,'
as she had called herself upon her trial, and was
known by in the prison books, was delegated to
the infirmary, where, before Daisy March's time

was up, she died—a poor, weak, wilful woman to the last, and resisting to the last all efforts to amend. It is the rule which governs innumerable lives like unto this, and which are ever drifting away, with good men, as it seems, powerless to save them; it is the dark cloud for ever lowering above the miles of roofs covering these ' prison homes,' and is charged with the lightning which destroys.

. Let us in our farewell chapters pass from this benighted land to a brighter scene beyond it. Here at least will be the moral to our story, the plain truth, as old as the green hills, that the ' ways of restoration ' are ' fashioned to the steps of ALL infirmity ;' and that the Great Hand is stretched forth to help all sinners striving to cross the border-land, separating the old life from the new, the false from true, the bad from good.

Seven years afterwards two women were seated, in the early evening of a summer's day, on the lawn of an old-fashioned garden, in one of the fairest portions of our Essex county. The church clock had struck six, but there were two hours at least of clear daylight in that bright midsummer time, and the heat of the day had disposed them both to linger there. They had been talking very earnestly—the younger woman seated on a lower seat at the feet of the elder, and looking up into her face with an earnest, wistful gaze, born of her deep affection.

Both women had served their apprenticeship to sorrow long ago, and looked before them now a trifle seriously, as if the ways of life were not all rose-strewn paths leading unto peace, whichever route the wayfarer might choose to strike out for himself. And one woman, the younger and fairer, had sinned and suffered and repented, and we know her still as Daisy March.

The elder, Miss Greenwood, of the Larches, 'down in Essex,'—she had come into a little property bequeathed her by Aunt Mary, and had retired from Government—was listening attentively to the remarks of her companion; for more of a companion than a lady's-maid, and more of a friend than either, had this prison waif become. The love and gratitude of Daisy March, the slowly failing health of Kate Greenwood, the strange tie of prison service, even in so different a fashion as the State had been served by each of them, had bound their hearts together very strongly, and the memorable past, though there were bitter records in it, was a link that time only riveted more closely.

Kate had worked hard for the redemption of a stubborn nature that had known sin, and been trained to it from the cradle side, but here was her reward at last, in the faithful reverence of her handmaiden, in the sweet knowledge that this soul had been saved from the darkness by her efforts, her encouragement, and her example, by that consideration for the 'fallen and degraded of our kind,' which had been at the heart of one good Christian, whom we have known as Patience Greenwood.

That Daisy March had become a perfect character in all respects, it would be a mistake to assert—the perfect beings exist not on this lower land. She had many faults, was not always patient under the little trials of life, as though some sparks of the old red fire of opposition were smouldering still within her; but she strove readily to make amends for all her petty faults of omission and commission, and at her heart was ever the deep sense of gratitude to set her right again, and the deeper conscious-ness of all that she had escaped, and all the peace and rest of the present life about her.

Still life had not ended yet, and Daisy March was only one-and-twenty years of age. There were trials and temptations yet to come—nay, had come, for Daisy was perplexed and almost fretful that day, and Kate Greenwood was acting as adviser on that summer evening when we first escape our prison world.

Daisy March had had an offer of marriage that very morning, and it had disturbed, perplexed, grieved her, and altogether had resulted in un-settling her from her usual train of calm, grave thoughts. It had come upon her unexpectedly too—which is not often the case in feminine history—but then Daisy March had never thought of marrying, or giving in marriage, knowing that the great, black past lay like a barrier between her and any honest man who might think what a fair young wife she would make him. The past was dead—and as she hoped from all memories irrevocably buried—but it was a reminiscence to her not to be lived down, and she would have no one in the better life about her dream of it, save the earnest, religious woman, whom she called her mistress.

Kate Greenwood still retained her gift of perspicacity—she was a strangely observant woman with the great art of not appearing to observe, and ill-health had not weakened her power in this respect.

'But you love this Robert Halstead, Daisy,' said the low voice of the mistress.

'Oh! I'm almost sure I don't,' cried Daisy, 'I—I have never thought of such a thing. And as for thinking that he, he—had it ever in his heart to think of me, I never could have fancied that. Oh! what made him so foolish,' cried Daisy, bursting into tears at last, 'when there were so many better girls about than I can ever be.'

'Still you love this Robert Halstead?' Kate persisted in asserting.

'I didn't,' cried Daisy.

'But you do now.'

'I—I don't know. I'm sure I don't though,' cried Daisy, very irrelevantly.

'And Robert Halstead loves you,' said Miss Greenwood, very thoughtfully, 'and that must be taken into consideration too, before we have quite made up our minds what to say, and Mr. Halstead comes here for your answer.'

'My answer is, No,' said Daisy, very firmly.

'You have made up your mind to that?'

'Yes, yes. Very decidedly, very firmly, I have made up my mind,' answered Daisy March, 'and, oh! my dear mistress, do not *you* try to turn me from it.'

'I will make no promise yet,' said Kate Greenwood, in reply.

'I shall think you are tired of me—that you want to get rid of me—or to tell *him* all the story of my guilty past,' cried Daisy.

'A past of which you have repented.'

'But which I would hide for ever from the world,' cried Daisy, 'which I will hide, or die—especially from him.'

'Hush, hush, this is extravagance, not reasoning,' reproved Kate Greenwood, 'and you do not know what is best.'

'Do you, Miss Kate?' was the rejoinder.

'Well—no, not yet,' confessed the mistress.

'I think I do—I'm sure I do,' said Daisy March, 'to thank Mr. Halstead for his offer, and say—I won't have him at any price!'

'What a reply! And he will ask your reasons.'

'I am not obliged to tell them.'

'He will try and find out for himself then, being a curious man.'

'No, no; I don't think he will do that.'

'He will wonder what offence he has given; whom you love better than he, or why you are afraid to share your life with him.'

'Ah, then,' said Daisy, with a sigh, 'he must wonder. That is all.'

'We will see,' murmured Miss Greenwood to herself.

'And he—Oh! here he comes. What shall I do? where shall I hide?' cried Daisy March, her fair face flushing very crimson. She had leaped to her feet, and would have run away into the house, had not Robert Halstead been too close upon her to allow of even a retreat moderately graceful. As it was, she stood by the side of her mistress's garden chair and looked down at the grass, as the lover came slowly to her side.

Robert Halstead was a man some ten years Daisy March's senior; and, therefore, had passed his thirtieth year. He was a stalwart young farmer, with an honest face that looked at the world in an undaunted fashion, and with a fearless outlook at it, which told—unless looks were deceptive in this instance—of much courage and self-reliance. Hardly a handsome face, and yet one which was worth a second glance for the determination it expressed.

He came towards them with but little sign of the bashful suitor in his mien; more like a man who expected an answer which would be favourable to his suit than one whose heart was failing him for fear.

'Well,' he said, in a clear, ringing voice, in which only an acute ear, such as Kate Greenwood's, might have detected a scarcely perceptible tremor; 'I hope you have made up your mind, Daisy.'

'Yes,' was Daisy's answer, and without looking into the steadfast grey eyes directed to her half-averted face, 'I have made up my mind to say it cannot be.'

'Cannot be!' he repeated, in a lower, deeper voice.

'Yes, cannot be,' Daisy responded again.

'May I ask——'

'Oh, no, no; don't ask me,' cried Daisy March at once; ' it was what my mistress said you would do, and I cannot bear it.'

'Ay,' he said, more firmly now, 'but it is what I have right to ask, I think. It is what every man has a right to ask before he goes away for good.'

Daisy Marsh wrung her hands silently together, but did not utter another word.

'I was mistaken, then, altogether,' he said. 'I was too rough and uncultivated a fellow, with his own way to make in the world, and with no right to think of a young wife until his place was more assured. Is that it?'

'No,' answered Daisy, quickly.

'I was too old for you, perhaps. Ten years are a long sight of time between man and woman, some people think; but it's all on the right side, and I——'

He stopped as Daisy turned away, dropped slowly to her mistress's side and buried her fair head on her shoulder.

'Tell him not to say any more. Ask him to go,' she murmured; 'I cannot bear it any longer!'

'Can you not trust him with the whole truth?' whispered Kate, in the agitated girl's ears, as Robert Halstead took one turn across the lawn with his strong hands clasped behind his back.

'For Heaven's sake, no,' cried Daisy; 'I would rather die—I have said so, and I mean it, —than tell him what I have been. Let him go his way.'

'Shall I tell him for you?'

'If you do, I will drown myself to-night,' cried Daisy March, with the old prison fever raging in her suddenly. It was awfully exemplified; here was the fire lighting up again, the 'break out,' threatening, and Kate Greenwood was dismayed and silenced.

It was not till Robert Halstead was coming back slowly to them that Kate found her voice to say:

'Trust me; he shall never know this secret from me.'

'Thank you,' murmured Daisy; 'but say something to him which will not—not make it seem so hard to both of us.'

'I will,' was the whisper back, 'and if I can.'

Robert Halstead was close upon them; he had thought out his own position now, and was prepared to speak again, and argue his case from a new stand-point, which he trusted might plead in his favour, but the lady of the Larches balked him by taking up the thread of the discussion, and acting at once as spokeswoman for her he wished to marry.

'Mr. Halstead,' she said, very calmly, 'I think, for this poor girl's sake, it is hardly fair to prolong a painful interview. She has made up her mind not to leave me, and I have no wish to part from her. It is unlikely that her life or mine will lie apart until death steps in between us.'

'Yes, women talk like that,' said Robert Halstead, bluntly, 'but they do not mean it very often. And you, Miss Greenwood, I should have thought a more sensible woman than to have talked like it at all.'

Miss Greenwood coloured at the reproof, but she went on, very calmly:

'And Daisy does not want to go away. She and I have lived together for years, and understand each other's ways as no two persons can understand each other, until fidelity, and truth, and real affection have been proved to be something more than words between them. And so Daisy will not leave me ever.'

'For ever is a long day, madam,' muttered Robert Halstead; 'and you will pardon me for saying so, but it appears to me that there is more of selfishness than love for Daisy March in keeping her with you, in binding her life so hard and fast to yours.'

'Yes, it is selfish from your view of it,' confessed Kate Greenwood; 'but Daisy March is selfish too, and finds her happiness in my quiet home. And,' she added, after a pause, 'she will always find it there, unless her heart misgives her at the eleventh hour.'

'Daisy,' cried Robert Halstead, 'say it does, girl!'

'No, no; it does not,' answered Daisy at this appeal.

'I am almost an invalid, and require careful attendance and much faithful service,' concluded Kate; 'and I should be wholly lost without this little friend of mine; and so she will not desert me. She is very grateful for the offer of your hand, but she has the courage to look you in the face now and say it is better you should part.'

Daisy looked up at this appeal, quick to respond to her own share in this hard deception.

'Yes, it is much the better for us all,' said Daisy, very firmly. 'I—I should not be happy with you.'

'I can say no more,' he answered, very sadly,

'save that I am dashed down completely, and that it is my own foolish fault.'

He held out his hand to Daisy, and wrung it in his own an instant; then he bowed more formally to Miss Greenwood, and went his way.

'Why have you made yourself so cruel in his eyes?' asked Daisy March, as the click of the wicket gate told that he had passed into the country road.

'I have been cruel to be kind,' was the enigmatic reply.

'But you have made yourself so—so unlike yourself,' said Daisy; 'and it was not what I wished.'

'I had a reason for it.'

'That he should not suspect there was a mystery, or that there had always been a blight about my wretched life?' cried Daisy.

'No, not that. And the life should be no longer wretched to one poor child who sinned from ignorance, and only wanted the right way shown her to amend. Such a life, Daisy, should be glorious, even now. Unless——'

'Unless!' echoed Daisy March.

'Unless you love this man very much indeed.'

'I love him too well to deceive him,' was the answer back, 'and I am very, very happy with you.'

'That's well.'

'And your reason for lowering yourself—for being so unlike my own true-hearted mistress—to this Robert Halstead?' asked Daisy March, returning to the old subject which had bewildered her, even in the rush of love-thoughts which had come to her brain.

'Ah! that I will tell you presently,' replied Miss Greenwood, with a smile.

The twilight was deepening on these figures as they walked towards the house, the stars were quivering over their heads. the sun had gone down in a glory of golden flame, and the night was close at hand. As they passed on together, there followed in the shadow of the bushes the shadow of their lives—a spectre from the old grim prison days—a wreck drifting still more hopelessly and wreck-like on the ocean of crime towards the barren shore on which it must break piecemeal. They had been tracked by this outcast of the prison. She had followed them and found them out with much cunning, acting by orders of men and women as .cunning as herself, and who were lurking in their dens of London and Liverpool unwilling to give up one clever child whose 'handy fingers' had done so much for the gang, and had resulted in such handsome profit. A genius, this Daisy March—and not to be allowed to quit her sphere of action without one more effort from father, mother, friends. Without a dozen efforts, if it were necessary, for that matter.

When the light was shining from the window of the little parlour, where the blind remained undrawn, and the window was left open for the sweet summer air to cool the room in which the two watched women sat, the watcher approached more stealthily, and took up her position where, in the distance, her keen sight could see them very clearly.

It was Janet Finlauson, the woman who had served her time out, and gone back to the old, bad life—the woman who of late days had made the acquaintance of the Marchs, and had heard them wondering what had become of a child more than ordinarily clever, and who would turn out a woman more than ordinarily clever too, and make a fortune with her ready wit and handsome face.

'I think as I can find her,' Janet had said.

'Tell her her mother is dying, and wants to see her bad,' suggested Mrs. March, who was very much intoxicated at that moment, and might be—possibly was—dying fast of the drink she took by wholesale now.

Janet had started on her expedition hopeful of finding her; and resolved to find her at all hazards—being pertinacious in all things evil, and when the evil days were free for her to act her worst. Still Janet was a strange woman in her way, and had one fault or virtue. She was prone to act on impulse—for good or for bad—and there were moments when she was hardly Janet Finlanson. As she approached the open window, with the noiseless step of a sleuth hound, there rang out clear and resonant in the summer air the words of Holy Writ—words of consolation and comfort to those stricken down, words of hope to those in suffering and sin, and of promise to the penitent, words which Janet Finlanson had heard in the prison chapel scores of times with deadened ears and heart, but which vibrated awfully within her that night. She stopped aghast, and went back a step or two, but still where the inmates of the room were not hidden from her view. She could see the well-known face of the matron bending over the open Bible, and with a bright look upon it that seemed hardly of the earth in that hour, and the rapt attention on a face more fair and young. The resignation and the trust expressed there, touched the woman on the watch—and such a woman!—with the live coal of a strong, if fitful remorse. She recoiled, and went further and further back into the ongathering night, flinging up once her arms despairingly, and as she had done seven years ago when a child of fourteen years of age was brought into the prison yard.

'No! I won't have nothink to do with it.

Not me!' were the last words of Janet Finlanson as she passed from the garden into the country road lying beyond.

CHAPTER VIII.

THE WHOLE TRUTH.

MISTRESS and ward had read far into the night before the Bible was closed, and they were regarding each other with looks of fair content. The timepiece on the mantel-shelf was striking eleven, a late hour for early Essex folk, as Kate Greenwood looked round astonished not a little at the progress of time.'

'So late as that,' exclaimed the mistress, 'I had no idea of it.'

She had been reading very long and earnestly; her extensive knowledge of the Scriptures had stood her in good stead, and enabled her to dwell upon innumerable passages which seemed, as it were, to have been written especially for souls stricken down as Daisy March's was that night, despite the strong, good fight she had made.

'Yes, it is late,' said Daisy, 'but go on.'

'Not now.'

'I am resigned,' Daisy March continued, 'and my duty lies with you for good. Every hour I see that very clearly.'

'I do not see it so clearly as yourself,' replied the elder woman, 'but I am very happy to think of your content, in time. And if you *will* be contented with my quiet life and ways.'

'I will,' responded Daisy March.

At the same moment there came to their ears the sound of footsteps on the lonely country road, and both of them paused to listen, even held their breath to listen. They were advancing rapidly, and to one pair of loving ears they were familiar footfalls.

'He is coming back. Oh! Miss Kate, he is coming back,' cried Daisy, 'what shall we do now, if he begins to talk again?'

'Who?'

' Robert Halstead. I am sure it is his step. I would know it in a thousand.'

' Strange !'

' What is he coming back for at this time of night ?' asked Daisy, trembling again.

' Courage,' replied Kate Greenwood, ' we shall see.'

They stood at the open window waiting and watching, and the footfalls came on nearer and nearer, approaching with strange haste. There was a sudden pause at the gate beyond, as if the lighted room were a surprise in its turn to him who was advancing, and then the figure of a man came across the lawn towards them.

' Is that you, Robert Halstead ?' called out Kate Greenwood.

' Yes, it is I—do not be afraid,' was the deep answer back, before Robert Halstead stood facing them once again.

' What is the matter ?' said both watchers at once, as they went back step by step into the room, followed by him who had evidently come in search of them.

' A woman has met with an accident crossing

the canal bridge, and has been carried to my farm,' said Robert Halstead.

'We can be of assistance, then,' said Kate. 'Shall we come at once? Has a doctor been sent for?'

'The doctor is there, but the woman wishes to see Miss Greenwood before the night is out.'

'Indeed!'

'Her name is Janet Finlanson, and you, Miss Greenwood, she says, will remember her as a prisoner once under your charge.'

'Yes,' replied Miss Greenwood, very calmly, 'I remember her very well.'

'You have been in prison service, then, Miss Greenwood?'

'I was a prison matron for three years or more,' was the answer back.

'I did not know that,' he said. Then he looked wistfully and very sorrowfully at her whom he had asked that day to be his wife, and added: 'I have not been trusted very much with the history of your lives, and I had no right to expect that you should tell it to me. Only——'

' Only,' repeated Daisy and Kate.

' Only you might have trusted me. It would have been so much the best.'

' Has Janet Finlanson said anything more?' asked Miss Greenwood.

' She is wild in her statements—altogether a strange and uncontrollable woman,' was his evasive answer; ' but she is anxious to see you both, to ask your forgiveness and advice. Put you both, as she says, on your guard.'

' Is she in danger?'

' There is no immediate danger.'

' I will go to her now. But why does she want to see Daisy?' inquired Kate Greenwood.

' She wishes to see you both, I have said. She has mentioned both your names,' answered the farmer, looking hard at Daisy.

' What—what has she said about me?' was asked now, in a troubled voice.

' She has told me all she knew,' he replied.

Daisy clasped her hands together for an instant, and then spread them before her face. Kate Greenwood came back from the doorway and stood beside the girl she had sheltered and saved; the protector to the last, if any help were needed.

'She has told you what I was?' murmured Daisy.

' Yes,' was the reply; ' but——'

' But you do not believe it,' said Daisy. 'Oh! it is true enough, God knows.'

' But it has made no difference in my thoughts of you,' he answered very earnestly; 'and that is what I was going to say when you interrupted me. Yes, I know all the story, Daisy; I have insisted upon knowing it, and it is a record of salvation surely. You stepped from darkness to light; you have repented. You began a new life here with this good woman at your side; you have made restitution.'

'I think you understand her now,' said Kate Greenwood, very softly.

' And it was for this, then, Daisy, that you would not become my wife?' he asked.

' I was unfit to be your wife, Robert. And I did not want you to guess what 1 had ever been,' she cried. 'I—I would so much rather have died than have had you know.'

'It is as well I do.'

He was leaning over her and endeavouring to draw her hands down from her face, but she resisted him. Kate Greenwood moved once more towards the door.

'I will get my bonnet on,' said she; and Robert Halstead looked gratefully towards her, when Daisy cried:

'Don't go; oh! don't go.'

Kate paused again; and Robert Halstead said:

'It is right you should remain for a minute or two longer, if you will.'

'Very well.' And Kate went back to the side of Daisy March; and once more the arm was passed round the neck of the weeping girl.

'I'm a rough fellow in my way, Daisy,' said Robert; 'and say things out very plainly, and I fear I have offended you.'

'No, no.'

'That's well. I am doubtful if I am a religious man,' he said, 'but I do not look back at the past of any man or woman if the present tells of a worthy and earnest life; and that is true religion, possibly.'

'It approaches it,' answered Miss Greenwood, 'but it is not religion.'

'What is it?' he asked, quickly.

'Charity.'

'And Mercy,' murmured Daisy March.

'Well, let it be Faith and Hope as well, or lead to them,' he answered. 'I am alone in the world, and without the world to take into consideration; and I am unhappy alone, and without you, Daisy. Let the past go back from us; you and I can look forward to the future, trusting in each other.'

'Can you ever trust me?' murmured Daisy.

'With all my heart, I will,' answered Robert Halstead.

'I must have time to think, to make up my mind,' said Daisy; 'it is all so like a dream to me. You know now, at least, that it was out of respect for you and your good name that I said No, to-night. I felt myself unworthy, though I dared not tell you so.'

'I thought you loved me a little, perhaps a

great deal, but Miss Greenwood threw me aback and confused me. I went away, madam,' he said, turning to Kate, 'thinking it was all your fault.'

'That is what I wanted you to think,' Kate answered; 'what I schemed for after my woman's fashion.'

Daisy looked up now, and for the first time.

Kate went on :

'I wanted you to think it was my selfishness that stood in the way, and not her affection. I wanted you to wait for her, to give her time ; to see, as time went on, that her heart was, after all, in your honest keeping. And I thought,' she added, ' that, in that good time, she might be led to tell you all the truth, and you to pardon it for her sake.'

'As I have done, at once. And if I have any right to pardon.'

' You will look not back to the past, but to the future, together.'

He took Daisy's hands in his, and she did not withdraw them from him now ; but she whispered, in a lower tone :

' That past is so terribly black !'

' But the future has the light of Heaven on it,' answered her lover.

' Heaven !' repeated Daisy March.

THE LUCK OF LUKE SHANDS.

THE LUCK OF LUKE SHANDS.

CHAPTER I.

MY LADY'S CHAPEL.

IT was a quaint little village that of Felspar. It is still a quaint village, although Felspar is famous in its way now, and has one big hotel in the valley, and by the stream which falls head-long from the hills to a boulder-broken channel, where the water fumes and froths and rushes by, a mass of seething silver in the sun. The hotel does well in the summer time, because there are curiosities in Felspar, and tourists and geologists come to see them; because there are fine bits of English hill scenery and woodland, pine-trees and white, weird tors, and artists come to paint them; because the guide-books have written up Felspar, and it is fashionable to see it, and fashionable folk, being sheep-like, come in droves in the season, with odd-looking shepherds to keep an eye upon them sometimes. But our story is of Felspar before it woke up, and found itself famous, and of a certain humble individual who helped to make it famous, and who, without a dream of greatness, fortunate fellow that he was, had greatness thrust upon him. There are some lucky people in the world —even of a world not lying back more than fifteen years from present date.

Fifteen years ago, then, Felspar was only known to a few in the county in which it was hiding, and to the people who lived and died in the little nest of cottages clustered by the one-arched stone bridge crossing the babbling brook; to the inhabitants of the bigger village ten miles away, and to a few folk in the nearest town, twenty miles off as the crow flies, the town that had a railway-station all to itself, and was a flourishing place, and had waters which cured gout and rheumatism and general bone-disarrangements, and was at all times and seasons running over with every variety of cripple and contortionist.

Felspar, fifteen years ago, was only running over with every variety of beauty—which it had completely, which those living in it day by day did not seem to value, for they were a homespun, matter-of-fact lot, whose only thought was how to live, but who clung to the place because their fathers and grandfathers had clung to it before them, struggling in the summer on a-few-shillings-a-week's wage to rear a large family—and rearing it!—and fighting with the winter always desperately, and dying in the fight now and then.

It was getting on for winter, when the days were cold and the nights set in very early in the Felspar valley, although the leaves had not shaken themselves off the trees, and there were rare autumnal tints about for those who cared to notice them, and nobody did care. 'Leaves brownish,' was the one verdict, and there was an end of it, just as in the City sometimes, 'money's tightish,' and then there is an end of that.

And yet, if anyone noticed the beauty of the autumn in the valley, it was Peggy Brantwell, a pretty girl acclimatised to much out-of-door occupation, with her grandfather's pigs and poultry to look after, and two cows to milk, and her grandfather to keep in a good temper, and make sure that his poor old legs took him up safely to bed in the early evening before ' a sight of candle-light ' was wasted. Peggy was a beauty in her way, or rather had been a beauty in her day, for she was seven-and-twenty now. She was a favourite with Felspar folk, who thought her grandfather was hard upon her, and put upon her, like an old curmudgeon as he was, they said, old Brantwell being as generally disliked as are most people who give themselves airs, and are better off than their neighbours. Why Peggy had grown up so amiable and lovable a little woman under the guardianship of Matthew Brantwell no one exactly could make out, and why, when it was rumoured he was not kind to her, and said hard things, and taunted and suspected her, and threatened her even with turning her out of house and home, she did not take him at his word, and get 'oop and oot o' it,' the Felspar community did not understand. But the Felspar community was not quick of comprehension; they were fully certain Peggy could have done better for herself than remaining all these years her grandfather's drudge—that Lady Glide up at the Hall would have been glad long ago to have had her for lady's-maid, and trained her for a lady's-maid; they did not think it possible that there could be any affection for an irritable, rasping, ungenerous old hunks who gave nobody a good word; she might be waiting for her grandfather's money—which, with his usual spirit of contrariness, he would be sure to leave elsewhere—but it was impossible to say what she *was* waiting for. Unless—she was waiting for Luke Shands, which we may say at once was exactly the fact of the case.

Perhaps, to put it more politely, it would have been graceful to say Luke Shands was waiting for her; but, as they were waiting for each other, it matters not a great deal, and looking at it either way is to look at it in the right light.

Matthew Brantwell, however, did not look at it in the right light at all; they were waiting till he was dead, he said; he was sure they were waiting till he was dead and gone, but he was not a-going to die to oblige either of them. His father had lived till ninety-four, and he was only seventy-three next bean-feast, and, bar his cussed legs, he was as good a man as any in Felspar, and, if they were waiting for his death and his money, never were two people more mistaken in their lives. As they would see, see if they wouldn't, rabbit 'em for a selfish, aggravating, greedy pair!

'But we are not waiting for your death, grandfather,' Peggy said, on the autumn day to which we have already alluded; 'I shall be only too glad if you'll live to be as old as Methusaleh.'

'I shouldn't be surprised if I did.'

'No,' said Peggy, laughing.

'There's been some wonderful ages in my

family. I don't see anything to laugh at in the idea,' said Mr. Brantwell.

'Oh, you're not an old man yet, grandfather,' said Peggy, as she bustled about the room preparing the afternoon tea for her relative. 'There are plenty in Felspar older than you, and plenty younger who look as old already.'

'Because they never took care of themselves,' he said, 'but sotted away their time at the "Quarry Inn," and sat up till nine or ten night after night, like them rackety Londoners. Because—but ain't you in a mortal hurry to get tea over to-night?'

'What a question!' said Peggy, briskly; 'is it any earlier?'

'It's a good bit earlier,' said her observant grandfather; 'the shadow across the floor was longer yesterday afternoon by fourteen inches afore the kettle biled.'

'I didn't notice the shadow,' said Peggy.

'But it was.'

'Indeed!'

'Very well—it was, then. And it was later in the afternoon, o' course. And you know it was later. And you had a reason for its being later yesterday, or earlier to-day, and it's no use trying to trick me,' he snapped.

' I am not trying to trick you, grandfather.'

' Yes, you are. You had a reason.'

· Well—I had a reason,' Peggy confessed.

' You're a-going out.'

' Yes—for a little while.'

' To meet that Luke. You know you are.'

' No, I'm not going to meet that Luke,' replied the grand-daughter. ' I'm not thinking of such a thing.'

' Oh, ain't you?' exclaimed the irritable old man, bringing his broad brown hand with a formidable slap into the tea-tray, and causing a considerable commotion amongst the crockery in consequence. ' Then why can't you be fair and straight, and say what you are going to do? Why can't you tell me you want to choke me off with tea before I've got the dinner down my throat, and to put me into bed again afore I'm hardly got out of it, or it's had time to cool? I hate such artful ways.'

' Grandfather, what has disturbed you to-day?'

'I ain't disturbed.'

'You are not very often like this.'

'Yes, I am.'

'Not often quite as hard as.this, I think,' said Peggy, in a calm, half-wondering way, which, if it had not been natural, would have been very aggravating. But Peggy was really surprised by the extra energy which her grandfather had contrived to throw into the conversation that afternoon.

'I shall be harder soon, if that's any comfort to you,' was the final remark of this amiable old gentleman; after which he went to bed, though the sun was still shining, and it was half an hour before his usual time. Indeed, the alacrity with which he had taken himself off would have aroused the suspicions of most folk; but Peggy was not distrustful—on the contrary, very, very trustful—or she would not have waited all this while for Luke Shands, and Luke Shands' luck, which was generally going the wrong way to which he was.

Five minutes after her grandfather had gone to bed, Peggy had put on her neat little straw hat, and was out of the house and tripping along the high-road. Had she looked back, she would have seen the head of old Matthew craning out of the front window watching her. Had she waited at the bend of the road, she would have found old Matthew there five minutes afterwards; and, had she hidden herself behind the great sprawling brambles, she would have seen Matthew bribe little Tom Crasp—a ragged youth, who professed to mind the sheep in Owen's fields, and spent his time in flinging stones at crows—to follow her, and bring him back the news where she had gone; to make all the haste he could too, because he, Matthew Brantwell, did not want to be out of his bed much later than his usual time.

But Peggy, unmindful of all this treachery, had gone on her way with grave composure, steadily and swiftly. She had turned from the high-road, or the apology that there was for a high-road in so break-neck a part of the country as Felspar, and gone down into the valley, deep down into the lower path by the side of the stream, where the trees arched overhead, and the way was thickly hidden now by rustling dead leaves.

Presently she crossed a little plank across the stream, and went up from the valley by degrees, making for the higher ground by a steep ascent through trees and bushes, which hid the way from those below. Here a hundred or a hundred and fifty feet from the valley's level, and a quarter of the way to the summit of the green-crested tor, she paused at a strange fissure in the rock, which she could now touch with her hands, and looked around at the fair English landscape lying beneath her steeped in autumn tints.

It had been a sharp ascent, and she might have paused to get her breath, only she was light of foot, and not half as 'blown' as Tom Crasp, who, lying on his stomach amongst the bracken, was panting like a puppy-dog.

Peggy Brantwell was waiting for something, it was evident. She crossed her hands, and sat down on a boulder that had slipped in times remote from the summit, and was covered now with lichens and mosses, and here she waited patiently, looking along the valley, a pretty figure that any artist would have loved to sketch. There was just a little expression of anxiety on her face even, as she gazed towards the sun dipping slowly behind a cloud-bank of purple and gold—a sun which she watched sink at last with all the devout expression of a fire-worshipper. Then, as the edge of the disc disappeared, she turned round, darted into the cleft of the rock, and was gone.

The cleft widened after a few steps over some rough, loose shingle, and here, well out of the draught, Peggy lighted a candle which she had brought with her, and went on groping her way steadily forward into the heart of those grand old cliffs, which have been the wonder of geologists of late years, but which no one thought a great deal about in Peggy's time.

Peggy's best time, that is—for Peggy lives and flourishes still, and has grown very stout and buxom, and laughs when she tells this story, as she has told it to the present writer—with all the fears and troubles in the background of some fifteen dusty years, and with the

sunshine, as she says, ' round about her everywhere.' And yet it was Peggy's best time, for
her good looks, and health and strength of
youth, and the faith and courage of love, and
in the belief even in old country superstitions,
which she clung to with the rest of the good
folk in Felspar, who believed in ' all the wonders,' just as unsophisticated Peggy did.

But Peggy was showing her belief by acts,
having great faith, poor little dreamer that she
was. And the proof was in this desperate expedition, and in the sudden dropping down on
her knees in a ragged, jagged part of the
cavern, which had widened out into some semblance of a rough-hewn room, and in planting
her candle on an anvil-shaped rock that stood
in the centre, uncommonly handy for catching
unawares the knee-caps of rash explorers. And
had anyone been listening, which there was not
—for Tom Crasp would not have followed her
into ' My Lady's Chapel ' for the wealth of
Felspar, and was even lurking outside with his
hair on end—he would have heard this extraordinary appeal to the hidden genius of the

place, supposed to be propitiatory to all inter-
cessions, if uttered five minutes after sundown,
neither more nor less, because her ladyship
loved punctuality, objected to be kept waiting,
and, it was possible, had important business
elsewhere :

' *Lady of the Grey Tor Chapel* (this repeated
three times), *listen to me, Peggy Brantwell, speaking with all her heart, as all must speak who enter
here, please bring luck to my dear Luke, change his
bad luck into good, and help us all you can. No
one has seen me come in, no one shall see me come
out. One, two, three, four, five, six, seven* (which,
being exactly the number of letters in Felspar,
was supposed to be the principal part of the
ceremony). *A, b, c, d* (to the end of the
alphabet). *High, low, Jack, game. Amen.*' Here
our superstitious heroine blew out her candle,
deposited it as a votive offering to the gods on
the extempore altar, and groped her way cautiously and timidly through the fissure to the daylight, which shone at last ahead of her, and
which she was so long in discovering that she
began to fear she had taken a wrong turning,

and was coming out at the other end of the world.

There was only twilight left, in fact, when she emerged from My Lady's Chapel, and it had not pierced very far into the shadows. It would be pitch dark night before she got home to her grandfather's, she was afraid. Never mind, she had succeeded in her mission, and perhaps luck would turn now. At all events, she had done her best to make it turn, and no one could blame her afterwards. And no one had seen her come out, and—Yah!

Peggy gave vent to a very substantial, unromantic, and high-pitched yell, for exactly in front of her, and evidently highly amused by her exit from the cave—'grinning like a goose' she called it afterwards, and in her hot indignation—was Luke Shands.

END OF THE FIRST VOLUME.

LONDON: DUNCAN MACDONALD, PRINTER, BLENHEIM HOUSE.